Betty Neels sadly pass
As one of our best-lov
will be greatly missed, both by her friends
at Mills & Boon and by her legions of
loyal readers around the world. Betty was a
prolific writer and has left a lasting legacy
through her heartwarming novels, and
she will always be remembered as a truly
delightful person who brought
great happiness to many.

This special collection of Betty's
best-loved books, are all available in
Large Print, making them an easier read
on your eyes, and ensuring you
won't miss any of the romance in
Betty's ever-popular novels.

The Betty Neels Large Print Collection

September 2007
Nanny by Chance
The Vicar's Daughter
Henrietta's Own Castle
The Hasty Marriage

October 2007
The End of the Rainbow
The Magic of Living
Roses and Champagne
Never While the
   Grass Grows

November 2007
Hannah
Heaven is Gentle
Once for All Time
Tangled Autumn

December 2007
No Need to Say Goodbye
Cruise to a Wedding
A Kind of Magic
The Final Touch

January 2008
A Match for Sister Maggy
A Winter Love Story
The Edge of Winter
The Fifth Day of Christmas

February 2008
Esmeralda
Grasp a Nettle
An Apple from Eve
At the End of the Day

March 2008
An Unlikely Romance
A Secret Infatuation
Dearest Love
When May Follows

April 2008
The Bachelor's Wedding
Fate Takes a Hand
The Right Kind of Girl
Marrying Mary

May 2008
Polly
A Kiss for Julie
The Fortunes of Francesca
Making Sure of Sarah

June 2008
An Innocent Bride
Discovering Daisy
A Good Wife
Matilda's Wedding

July 2008
Always and Forever
An Independent Woman
Dearest Eulalia &
The Doctor's Girl
Emma's Wedding

DEAREST EULALIA

&

THE DOCTOR'S GIRL

BY

BETTY NEELS

MILLS & BOON®

Pure reading pleasure™

DEAREST EULALIA
First Published in Great Britain in 2000
THE DOCTOR'S GIRL
First Published in Great Britain in 2001
Large Print Edition 2008
Harlequin Mills & Boon Limited,
Eton House, 18-24 Paradise Road,
Richmond, Surrey TW9 1SR

DEAREST EULALIA © Betty Neels 2000
THE DOCTOR'S GIRL © Betty Neels 2001

ISBN: 978 0 263 20465 0

Set in Times Roman 16½ on 21 pt.
32-0708-57356

Printed and bound in Great Britain
by Antony Rowe Ltd, Chippenham, Wiltshire

CONTENTS

DEAREST EULALIA

CHAPTER ONE

THE two men talking together at the back of the hospital entrance hall paused to watch a young woman cross the vast floor. She was walking briskly, which suggested that she knew just where she was going, but she paused for a moment to speak to one of the porters and they had the chance to study her at their leisure.

She was worth studying: a quantity of dark brown hair framed a beautiful face and the nylon overall she was wearing couldn't disguise her splendid figure.

'Eulalia Langley,' said the elder of the two men, 'runs the canteen in Outpatients. Good at it, too. Lives with her grandfather, old Colonel

Langley—your father knew him, Aderik. No money, lives in a splendid house somewhere behind Cheyne Walk. Some family arrangement makes it impossible for him to sell it—has to pass it on to a nephew. A millstone round his neck; Eulalia lives with him, keeps the home going. She's been with us for several years now. Ought to have married by now but I don't suppose there's much chance of that. It's a full-time job here and there isn't much of the day left by the time the canteen shuts down.'

His companion said quietly, 'She's very beautiful,' and then added, 'You say that my father knew Colonel Langley?'

He watched the girl go on her way and then turned to his companion. He was tall and heavily built, and towered over his informative colleague. A handsome man in his thirties, he had pale hair already streaked with grey, a high-bridged nose above a thin mouth and heavy-lidded blue eyes. His voice held only faint interest.

'Yes—during the Second World War. They saw a good deal of each other over the years. I don't think you ever met him? Peppery man, and I gather from what I hear that he is housebound with severe arthritis and is now even more peppery.'

'Understandably. Shall I see more of you before I go back to Holland?'

'I hope you'll find time to come to dinner; Dora will want to see you and ask after your mother. You're going to Edinburgh this evening?'

'Yes, but I should be back here tomorrow—I'm operating and there's an Outpatient clinic I must fit in before I return.'

'Then I'll give you a ring.' The older man smiled. 'You are making quite a name for yourself, Aderik, just as your father did.'

Eulalia, unaware of this conversation, went on her way through the hospital to the Outpatients department, already filling up for the morning clinic.

It was a vast place, with rows of wooden

benches and noisy old-fashioned radiators which did little to dispel the chill of early winter. Although a good deal of St Chad's had been brought up to date, and that in the teeth of official efforts to close it, there wasn't enough money to spend on the department so its walls remained that particular green so beloved by authority, its benches scuffed and stained and its linoleum floor, once green like the walls, now faded to no colour at all.

Whatever its shortcomings, they were greatly mitigated by the canteen counter which occupied the vast wall, covered in cheerful plastic and nicely set out with piles of plates, cups and saucers, soup mugs, spoons, knives and paper serviettes.

Eulalia saw with satisfaction that Sue and Polly were filling the tea urn and the sugar bowls. The first of the patients were already coming in although the first clinic wouldn't open for another hour, but Outpatients, for all its drawbacks, was for many of the patients a sight better than cold bedsitters and loneliness.

Eulalia had seen that from the first moment of starting her job and since then, for four years, she had fought, splendid white tooth and nail, for the small comforts which would turn the unwelcoming place into somewhere in which the hours of waiting could be borne in some degree of comfort.

Since there had been no money to modernise the place, she had concentrated on the canteen, turning it by degrees into a buffet serving cheap, filling food, soup and drinks, served in brightly coloured crockery by cheerful, chatty helpers.

With an eye on the increasing flow of patients, she sent two of the girls to coffee and went to check the soup. The early morning clinic was chests, and that meant any number of elderly people who lived in damp and chilly rooms and never had quite enough to eat. Soup, even so early in the morning, would be welcome, washed down by strong tea…

One clinic succeeded another; frequently two or more ran consecutively, but by six o'clock the place was silent. Eulalia, after doing a last careful check, locked up, handed over the keys to the head porter and went home.

It was a long journey across the city but the first surge of home-goers had left so she had a seat in the bus and she walked for the last ten minutes or so, glad of the exercise, making her way through the quieter streets down towards the river until she reached a terrace of imposing houses in a narrow, tree-lined street.

Going up the steps to a front door, she glanced down at the basement. The curtains were drawn but she could see that there was a light there, for Jane would be getting supper. Eulalia put her key in the door and opened the inner door to the hall, lighted by a lamp on a side table—a handsome marble-topped nineteenth-century piece which, sadly, her grandfather was unable to sell since it was all part and parcel of the family arrangement…

There was a rather grand staircase at the end of the hall and doors on either side, but she passed them and went through the green baize door at the end of the hall and down the small staircase to the basement.

The kitchen was large with a large old-fashioned dresser along one wall, a scrubbed table at its centre and a Rayburn cooker, very much the worse for wear. But it was warm and something smelled delicious.

Eulalia wrinkled her beautiful nose. 'Toad-in-the-hole? Roasted onions?'

The small round woman peeling apples at the table turned to look at her.

'There you are, Miss Lally. The kettle's on the boil; I'll make you a nice cup of tea in a couple of shakes. The Colonel had his two hours ago.'

'I'll take a cup of tea with me, Jane; he'll be wanting his whisky. Then I'll come and give you a hand.'

She poured her own tea, and put a mug beside Jane. 'Has Grandfather had a good day?'

'He had a letter that upset him, Miss Lally.' Jane's nice elderly face looked worried. 'You know how it is; something bothers him and he gets that upset.'

'I'll go and sit with him for a bit.' Eulalia swallowed the rest of her tea, paused to stroke Dickens, the cat, asleep by the stove, and made her way upstairs.

The Colonel had a room on the first floor of the house at the front. It was a handsome apartment furnished with heavy mahogany pieces of the Victorian period. They had been his grandparents' and although the other rooms were furnished mostly with Regency pieces he loved the solid bulk of wardrobe, dressing table and vast tallboy.

He was sitting in his chair by the gas fire, reading, when she tapped on the door and went in.

He turned his bony old face with its formidable nose towards her and put his book down.

'Lally—jut in time to pour my whisky. Come and sit down and tell me about your day.'

She gave him his drink and sat down on a cross-framed stool, its tapestry almost threadbare, and gave him a light-hearted account of it, making much of its lighter moments. But although he chuckled from time to time he was unusually silent, so that presently she asked, 'Something's wrong, Grandfather?'

'Nothing for you to worry your pretty head about, Lally. Stocks and shares aren't a woman's business and it is merely a temporary setback.'

Lally murmured soothingly. Grandfather belonged to the generation which considered that women had nothing to do with a man's world, and it was rather late in the day to argue with him about that.

She said cheerfully into the little silence, 'Jane and I were only saying this morning that it was a waste of gas and electricity keeping the drawing room open. I never go in there, and if anyone comes to call we can use the morning room…'

'I'll not have you living in the kitchen,' said the Colonel tetchily.

'Well, of course not,' agreed Lally cheerfully, and thought how easy it was to tell fibs once she got started. 'But you must agree that the drawing room takes a lot of time to get warm even with the central heating on all day. We could cut it down for a few hours.'

He agreed reluctantly and she heaved a sigh of relief. The drawing room had been unheated for weeks and so, in fact, had most of the rooms in the house; only her grandfather's room was warm, as was the small passage leading to an equally warm bathroom. Lally wasn't deceitful but needs must when the devil drove…

She went back to the kitchen presently and ate her supper with Jane while they planned and plotted ways and means of cutting down expenses.

It was ridiculous, thought Eulalia, that they

had to go on living in this big house just because some ancestor had arranged matters to please himself. Her grandfather couldn't even let it to anyone; he must live in it until he died and pass it on to a nephew who lived on the other side of the world. The family solicitor had done his best but the law, however quaint, was the law. Trusts, however ancient, couldn't be overset unless one was prepared to spend a great deal of money and probably years of learned arguing...

Eulalia ate her supper, helped Jane tidy the kitchen and observed with satisfaction that tomorrow was Saturday.

'I'll get Grandfather into his chair and then do the shopping.'

She frowned as she spoke; pay day was still a week away and the housekeeping purse was almost empty. The Colonel's pension was just enough to pay for the maintenance of the house and Jane's wages; her own wages paid for food and what Jane called keeping up appearances.

What we need, reflected Eulalia, is a miracle. And one was about to happen.

There was no sign of it in the morning, though. Jane was upstairs making the beds, the Colonel had been heaved from his bed and sat in his chair and Eulalia had loaded the washing machine and sat down to make a shopping list. Breast of chicken for the Colonel, macaroni cheese for Jane and herself, tea, sugar, butter… She was debating the merits of steak and kidney pudding over those of a casserole when the washing machine, long past its prime, came to a shuddering stop.

Usually it responded to a thump, even a sharp kick, but this morning it remained ominously silent. Extreme measures must be taken, decided Eulalia, and searched for a spanner—a useful tool she had discovered when there was no money for a plumber…

Mr van der Leurs, unaware that he was the miracle Eulalia wished for, paid off his taxi and

made his way to the Colonel's house. A man es-
teemed by the members of his profession,
renowned for his brilliant surgery, relentlessly
pursued by ladies anxious to marry him, he had
remained heart-whole, aware that somewhere on
this earth there was the woman he would love
and marry and until then he would bury his handsome nose in work. But his patience had been re-
warded; one glimpse of Eulalia and he knew that
he had found that woman. Now all he had to do
was to marry her…

He reached the house and rang the bell and
presently the door was opened and Eulalia stood
there in a grubby pinny, looking cross. She still
had the spanner in her hand, too. He saw that he
would need to treat her with the same care with
which he treated the more fractious of his small
patients.

His 'Good morning' was briskly friendly. 'This
is Colonel Langley's house? I wondered if I
might visit him? My father was an old friend of

his—van der Leurs.' He held out a hand. 'I am
Aderik van der Leurs, his son.'

Eulalia offered a hand rather reluctantly.
'Grandfather has talked about a Professor van
der Leurs he met years ago...'

Mr van der Leurs watched her face and read
her thoughts accurately.

'I'm visiting at St Chad's for a few days,' he
told her. 'Mr Curtis mentioned that the Colonel
was housebound with arthritis and might be
glad to have a visit. I have called at an awkward
time, perhaps...'

He must be all right if Mr Curtis knew him, decided Eulalia.

'I think Grandfather would be pleased to see
you. Come in; I'll take you to his room.'

She led him across the hall but before she
reached the staircase she turned to look at him.

'I suppose you wouldn't know how to make a
washing machine start again?'

He had been wondering about the spanner. He

said with just the right amount of doubt in his voice, 'Shall I take a look?'

She led him into the kitchen and Mr van der Leurs gave his full attention to the machine just as though it were one of his small patients on the operating table awaiting his skill. After a moment he took the spanner from her hand, tapped the dial very very gently and rotated it. The machine gave a gurgle and when he tapped it again—the mere whisper of a tap—it came to life with a heartening swish.

Eulalia heaved a sigh of relief. 'Thank you very much. How clever of you, but I dare say you know something about washing machines.' She added doubtfully, 'But you're a doctor.'

He didn't correct her. 'I'm glad I could be of help,' he said, and then stood looking at her with a look of faint enquiry.

She said quickly, 'I'll take you to see Grand-father. He loves to have visitors.'

She took off her pinny and led the way into the

hall and up the graceful staircase. It was a cold house—although there were radiators along the walls, none of them gave warmth. Outside the Colonel's door Eulalia stopped. 'I'll bring coffee up presently—you'll stay for that?'

'If I may.'

She knocked and opened the door and then led him into the large room, pleasantly warm with a bright gas fire. There was a bed at one end of the room, bookshelves and a table by the wide window and several comfortable chairs. The Colonel sat in one of them, a reading lamp on the small table beside him, but he looked up as they went in. He eyed Mr van der Leurs for a moment. 'The spitting image of your father,' he observed. 'This is indeed a surprise—a delightful one, I might add.'

Mr van der Leurs crossed the room and gently shook the old hand with its swollen joints. 'A delight for me too, sir; Father talked of you a great deal.'

'Sit down if you can spare an hour. Lally, would you bring us coffee? You have met each other, of course?'

'Yes, Grandpa, I'll fetch the coffee.'

Mr van der Leurs watched her go out of the room. She wasn't only beautiful, he reflected, she was charming and her voice was quiet. He sat down near the Colonel, noting that the radiators under the window were giving off a generous warmth. This room might be the epitome of warmth and comfort but that couldn't be said of the rest of the house.

Eulalia, going back to the kitchen, wondered about their visitor. He had said that he was at St Chad's. A new appointment? she wondered. Usually such news filtered down to the canteen sooner or later but she had heard nothing. In any case it was most unlikely that she would see him there. Consultants came to Outpatients, of course, but their consulting rooms were at the other end and they certainly never went near the canteen. Perhaps he was visiting to give lectures.

She ground the coffee beans they kept especially for her grandfather and got out the coffee pot and the china cups and saucers, and while she arranged them on a tray she thought about Mr van der Leurs.

He was a handsome man but not so very young, she decided. He had nice blue eyes and a slow smile which made him look younger than he was. He was a big man and tall but since she was a tall girl and splendidly built she found nothing unusual about that. Indeed, it was pleasant to look up to someone instead of trying to shrink her person.

She found the Bath Oliver biscuits and arranged them on a pretty little plate and bore the tray upstairs and found the two men in deep conversation. The Colonel was obviously enjoying his visitor and she beamed at him as she handed him his coffee and put the biscuits where her grandfather could reach them easily. She went away then, nursing a little glow of pleasure because Mr van der Leurs had got up when she had gone in and taken the tray and stayed on his feet until she had gone.

Nice manners, thought Eulalia as she went downstairs to have her coffee with Jane.

'I heard voices,' observed Jane, spooning instant coffee into mugs.

Eulalia explained. 'And Grandfather was pleased to see him.'

'He sounds all right. I remember his dad; came visiting years ago.'

'He got the washing machine to go again.'

'That's a mercy. Now, Miss Lally, you do your shopping; I'll hang out the washing—see if you can get a couple of those small lamb cutlets for the Colonel and a bit of steak for us—or mince. I'll make a casserole for us and a pie if there's enough...'

Eulalia got her coat from the hall and fetched a basket and sat down at the table to count the contents of her purse. A week to pay day so funds were low.

'It had better be mince,' she said. 'It's cheaper.' And then she added, 'I hate mince...'

She looked up and saw that Jane was smiling—not at her but at someone behind her. Mr van der Leurs was standing in the doorway holding the coffee tray.

'Delicious coffee,' he observed, 'and I was delighted to meet the Colonel.'

Eulalia got up and turned round to face him. 'Thank you for bringing down the tray. This is Jane, our housekeeper and friend.'

He crossed the room and shook hands with her and smiled his slow smile so that she lost her elderly heart to him.

'Miss Lally's just going to do the shopping,' she told him.

'Perhaps I may be allowed to carry the basket?'

And very much to her surprise Eulalia found herself walking out of the house with him and down a narrow side street where there was a row of small shops, old-fashioned and tucked discreetly behind the rather grand houses.

She asked, 'Don't you have to go back to the

hospital? I mean, this is kind of you but you don't have to.'

'It's more or less on my way,' said Mr van der Leurs, and since she was too polite to ask where he was going and he had no intention of telling her she made polite small talk until they reached the shops.

The grocer's was small and rather dark but he sold everything. Mr van der Leurs, without appearing to do so, noted that she bought Earl Grey, the finest coffee beans, Bath Olivers, farm butter, Brie and Port Salut cheese, Cooper's marmalade and a few slices of the finest bacon; and, these bought, she added cheap tea bags, a tin of instant coffee, a butter substitute, sugar and flour and streaky bacon.

It was the same at the butcher's, where she bought lamb cutlets, a chicken breast, lamb's kidneys and then minced beef and some sausages. He hadn't gone into the shop with her but had stood outside, apparently studying the contents of the window. At the greengrocer's he followed her in to take the basket while she bought potatoes and a cabbage, celery, carrots and a bunch of grapes.

'We make our own bread,' said Eulalia, by-passing the baker.

Mr van der Leurs, keeping his thoughts to himself, made light-hearted conversation as they returned to the house. It was evident to him that living was on two levels in the Colonel's house, which made it a sensible reason for him to marry her as quickly as possible. There were, of course, other reasons, but those, like his thoughts, he kept to himself.

At the house he didn't go in but as he handed over the basket he said, 'Will you have lunch with me tomorrow? We might drive out into the country. I find the weekends lonely.'

It was a good thing that his numerous friends in London hadn't heard him say that. He had sounded very matter-of-fact about it, which somehow made her feel sorry for him. A stranger in a foreign land, thought Eulalia, ignoring the absurd idea; he seemed perfectly at home in London and his English was as good as her own.

'Thank you, I should like that.'

'I'll call for you about eleven o'clock.' He smiled at her. 'Goodbye, Eulalia.'

Jane thought it was a splendid idea. 'Time you had a bit of fun,' she observed, 'and a good meal out somewhere posh.'

'It will probably be in a pub,' answered Eulalia. She told her grandfather when she carried up his lunch.

'Splendid, my dear; he's a sound chap, just like his father was. I've asked him to come and see me again. He tells me he is frequently in England although he has his home in Holland.'

Eulalia, getting the tea later while Jane had a rest, spent an agreeable hour deciding what she would wear. It was nearing the end of October but the fine weather had held although it was crisply cold morning and evening. She decided on a short jacket, a pleated skirt and a silk jersey top, all of them old but because they had been expensive and well cut they presented an elegant whole. He had said that they would drive into the country, which might mean a pub lunch, but if it were to be somewhere grander she would pass muster...

When he called for her he was wearing beautifully cut tweeds, by no means new but bearing the hallmark of a master tailor, and his polished shoes were handmade. Even to an untutored eye he looked exactly what he was—a man of good taste and with the means to indulge it. Moreover, reflected Eulalia happily, her own outfit matched his.

He went to see her grandfather, to spend ten minutes with him and give him a book they had been discussing, and then stopped to talk to Jane, who was hovering in the hall, before he swept Eulalia out of the house and into the dark grey Bentley parked on the kerb.

'Is this yours?' asked Eulalia.

'Yes. I need to get around when I'm over here.'
He glanced at her. 'Comfortable? Warm
enough? It's a lovely morning but there's a nip
in the air.'

He took the M4 out of London and turned off
at Maidenhead. 'I thought the Cotswolds? We
could lunch at Woodstock and drive on from
there. A charming part of England, isn't it? You
don't need to hurry back?'

'No. Jane likes to go to Evensong but I expect
we shall be back long before then. Do you know
this part of England well?'

'Not as well as I should like but each time I
come here I explore a little more.'

He had turned off the A423 and was driving
along country roads, through small villages and
the quiet countryside to stop presently at North
Stoke, a village by the Thames where they had
coffee at a quiet pub. He talked quietly as he
drove, undemanding, a placid flow of nothing

much. By the time they reached Woodstock, Eulalia was wishing the day would go on for ever.

The Feathers was warm and welcoming, with a pleasant bar and a charming restaurant. Eulalia, invited to choose her lunch, gulped at the prices and then, urged by her companion, decided on lobster patties and then a traditional Sunday lunch—roast beef, Yorkshire pudding, roast potatoes, vegetables…and after that a trifle to put to shame any other trifle. Eulalia finally sighed with repletion and poured the coffee.

'What a heavenly meal,' she observed. 'I shall remember it for years.'

'Good. The Cotswolds are at their best in the autumn, I think.'

He drove to Shipton-under-Wychwood, on to Stow-on-the-Wold and then Bourton-on-the-Water where he obligingly stopped for a while so that she might enjoy its charm and the little river running through the village. At Burford he stopped for tea at a hotel in its steep main street, a warm and cosy place where they sat in a pleasant room by the fire and ate toasted teacakes oozing butter and drank the finest Assam tea.

'This is bliss,' said Eulalia, mopping a buttery mouth. She smiled at him across the little table. 'I've had a heavenly day. Now we have to go back, don't we?'

'I'm afraid so. I'll settle up and see you at the car.'

Eulalia, powdering her beautiful nose, made a face at her reflection.

This has been a treat, she told herself. It isn't likely to happen again and so I mustn't like him too much. Even if I were to meet him at St Chad's it wouldn't be the same; he might not even recognise me. He'll go back to Holland and forget me.

It was already getting dusk and this time Mr van der Leurs took the main roads, travelling at a steady fast pace while they carried on an easy flow of small talk. But for all that, thought Eulalia as they were once more enclosed by the city's suburbs, she still knew almost nothing about him. Not that that mattered since she was unlikely to see him again. She hadn't asked him when he was going back to Holland but she supposed that it would be soon.

At the house, he came in with her. They were met by Jane in the hall.

'You'll have had your tea, but the kettle's boiling if you'd like another cup. The Colonel's nicely settled until supper time. I'm off to church.'

She smiled at them both. 'You've had a nice day?'

'Oh, Jane, it was heavenly.'

'I thought it might be. I'll get my hat and coat.'

'I don't suppose you want more tea?' Eulalia asked Aderik.

'I'd love a cup. While you are getting it may I have five minutes with the Colonel?'

'He'd like that. Do you want me to come up with you?'

'No, no. I know my way. I won't stay more than a few minutes.'

He went up the staircase, tapped on the Colonel's door and, bidden to enter, did so.

The Colonel was sitting in his chair doing a jigsaw puzzle but he pushed it to one side when Mr van der Leurs went in.

'Aderik. You had a pleasant day? Where did you go?'

Mr van der Leurs sat down beside him and gave him a succinct account of the day.

'You found Lally good company? She goes out so seldom. Never complains but it's no life for a girl. I do wonder what will happen to her when I am no longer here. She can't stay here— the place has to go to a nephew. A good chap but married with children.'

'Perhaps I can put your mind at rest about that, sir. I intend to marry Eulalia.'

The Colonel stared at him and then slowly smiled. 'Not wasted much time, have you?'

'I'm thirty-eight. Those years have been wasted romantically. I fell in love with her when

I first saw her at St Chad's a day or two ago. I
see no reason to waste any more time. You have
no objection?'

'Good Lord, no. And your father would have
liked her, as I'm sure your mother will.' He paused
to think. 'She has no idea of your intentions?'

'None.'

'Well, I'm sure you know how you intend to go
about that. You have lifted a load off my mind,
Aderik. She's a dear girl and she has a loving heart.'

Mr van der Leurs got up and the Colonel offered a hand. 'You'll stay for supper?'

'No. I think not; enough is as good as a feast.
Is that not so?'

The colonel rumbled with laughter. 'You're
very like your father. Goodnight, my boy.'

Eulalia was in the kitchen. She and Jane were to
have jacket potatoes for their supper but it was
hardly a dish to offer to a guest. She hadn't asked
him to stay to supper but she expected him to.

She made the tea and when he entered the kitchen gave him a worried look.

'Shall we have tea here? Would you like to stay for supper?' She didn't sound at all eager and he hid a smile.

'Thank you but I mustn't stay. I've an appointment this evening. Tea would be fine.'

He drank his tea, waved aside her thanks for her day out, bade her a brisk goodbye and drove himself away. Eulalia shut the door as the Bentley slipped away, feeling hurt and a little peevish. He could at least have waved; it was almost as if he couldn't get away fast enough.

She poured herself another cup of tea. Of course he might be late for his appointment— with a girl? She allowed her imagination to run riot and then told herself sternly to stop being a fool. He was almost a stranger; she had only met him a couple of times; she knew nothing about him… So why was it that she felt so at ease with him, as though she had known him all her life?

If she had hoped to see him at the hospital the next day, she was disappointed. Her journeys into the hospital proper were limited to her visits to the supply department, the general office for requisitioning something for the canteen or taking money from the canteen at the end of the day to one of the clerical staff to lock away, but those trips took her nowhere near the wards and, since she had no idea as to what he actually did, even if she had the opportunity she had no idea where to look for him.

Filling rolls with cheese as the first of the day's patients began to surge in, she told herself to forget him.

Since it was the haematology outpatients clinic the benches were filling up fast. She recognised several of the patients as she poured tea and offered rolls. Anaemia in its many guises took a long time to cure, and if not to cure at least to check for as long as possible...

The clinic was due to start at any moment. She

glanced towards the end of the waiting room to the row of consulting rooms and almost dropped the teapot she was filling. Mr van der Leurs, enormous in a white coat, was going into the first room, flanked by two young doctors and a nurse.

'But he's a mister,' said Eulalia to the teapot. 'A surgeon, so why is he at this clinic?' She had picked up quite a bit of knowledge since she had been working at St Chad's, not all of it accurate but she was sure that haematology was a medical field. He had disappeared, of course, and he wouldn't have seen her.

In this she was mistaken.

When the clinic was finally over she was at the back of the canteen getting ready for the afternoon's work and didn't see him leave.

It was six o'clock by the time she had closed the canteen, checked the takings and locked up. She got into her coat, picked up the bag of money and went through to the hospital. The clerk on night duty would lock it away and she would be free to go home. It was a pity that she had seen Mr van der Leurs again, she reflected. It had unsettled her.

She handed over the money and made for the main door. With any luck she wouldn't have to wait too long for a bus and the rush hour was over.

She pushed open the swing doors and walked full tilt into Mr van der Leurs.

He said easily, 'Ah, Eulalia, I was on my way to look for you. I have a book for your grandfather and I wondered if you would like a lift?'

She said slowly, 'I saw you in Outpatients this morning. I thought you were a surgeon—Mr, you know?'

He had taken her arm and was leading her to where the Bentley was parked.

'I am a surgeon, but I do a good deal of bone marrow transplanting and I had been asked to take a look at several patients who might benefit from that.'

He popped her into the car, got in beside her and drove away.

Eulalia said, 'Oh, I see,' which wasn't very adequate as a reply but it was all she could think of, and she answered his casual enquiry as to her day just as briefly; she hadn't expected to see him again and it had taken her by surprise.

He went straight up to the Colonel's room when they reached the house and when he came down again after ten minutes or so she was in the hall. There wasn't a fire in the drawing room. If he accepted her offer of coffee he would have to drink it in the kitchen; the drawing room would be icy...

He refused her offer. 'I'm leaving for Holland in the morning,' he told her, then he smiled down at her, shook her hand, and was gone.

CHAPTER TWO

JANE came to the kitchen door. 'Gone, has he?
Well, it was shepherd's pie for supper; I doubt if
he would have fancied that. I'll get a tin of
salmon in the house; if he comes again, unexpected, like, I can make fishcakes.'

Eulalia said quietly, 'No need, Jane; he's going
back to Holland in the morning.'

'You'll miss him…'

'I don't really know him, but yes, I shall miss
him.'

Which was exactly what Mr van der Leurs
had hoped for.

She was pouring tea for the thirsty queue towards
the end of Thursday's afternoon clinic when she

looked up and saw him. She put the teapot down with a thump and hoped that she didn't look as pleased as she felt; he had, after all, bidden her goodbye without a backward glance...

The queue parted for him to watch and listen with interest.

'I'll be outside the entrance,' he told her, smiled impartially at the queue and went on his way.

"E was 'ere last week,' said a voice. 'Looking at my Jimmy—ever so nice 'e was, too.'

'A friend of yours, miss?' asked another voice.

'An acquaintance,' said Eulalia in a voice which forbade confidences of any sort, her colour somewhat heightened. The queue dissolved, the last few patients were called, she began to clear up, and presently, the hall empty, Sue and Polly gone, she closed down for the day.

The clerk kept her talking when she took the money to the office. He was an elderly man and night duty was a lonely job and she was too kind and polite to show impatience while he talked. Perhaps Mr van der Leurs would think that she didn't intend to meet him. She hadn't said that she would, had she? And if it had been a casual offer made on the spur of the moment, he might not wait.

He was there, leaning against the Bentley's bonnet, oblivious of the chilly evening. He opened the door for her as she reached him and got in beside her.

'Could we go somewhere for a cup of coffee? I haven't much time...'

'You can have coffee at home—' began Eulalia, and was cut short by his curt,

'There's a café in the Fulham Road; that is the quickest way.'

She said tartly, 'If you are so pressed for time you had no need to give me a lift.'

He didn't answer but drove through the city. The café he ushered her into was small and half empty. He sat her down at a table away from the other customers, ordered coffee and observed in a matter-of-fact voice, 'This isn't quite what I intended but it will have to do. I got held up.'

The coffee came and Eulalia took a sip. 'I thought you were in Holland.'

'I was; I came over on the fast ferry this afternoon. I must go back on the ferry from Dover in a couple of hours' time.'

'You mean you're only here for an hour or two? Whatever for?'

'I wanted to see you and as I'm going to be away for a few days…'

'But you could have seen me at home or at the hospital.'

'Don't interrupt, Eulalia; there isn't time. It is enough to say that I wanted to see you alone.'

He smiled then and sat back, quite at his ease. 'Will you marry me, Eulalia?'

She opened her pretty mouth and closed it again and stared at him, sitting there asking her to marry him in a manner one would use to ask for the sugar.

'No,' said Eulalia.

He didn't look in the least put out. 'There are a dozen reasons why you should say no. Perhaps you will think about them while I'm away and when I see you again we can discuss them.' He smiled at her. 'I shall see you again, you know, and next time we can talk at our leisure. Now I'm afraid I must take you home.'

Eulalia could think of nothing to say; she tried out several sensible remarks to make in her head but didn't utter them. She could, of course, tell him that she didn't want to see him again but somehow she didn't say so. Later she would think of all kinds of clever replies to make but he wouldn't be there to hear them. And she musn't see him again.

He drove the short distance to the Colonel's house, got out and went with her to the door.

'Well, goodbye,' said Eulalia, and offered a hand.

'Not goodbye; we say *tot ziens*.' He shook her hand briefly and opened the door for her.

As he turned away she asked, 'Where are you going?'

'Albania.'

'But that's... Oh, do take care!'

He stood looking down at her for a moment, his eyes half hidden under their heavy lids. Just for a moment Eulalia had let her heart speak for itself.

Driving down to Dover and once on the other side of the Channel, taking the long road home, Mr van der Leurs allowed his thoughts to dwell on a pleasant future.

October became November and brought cold wind and rain and grey skies, none of which lightened Eulalia's mood. Mr van der Leurs had been gone for a week and she worried about him, and although she told herself that he was old enough and large enough to take care of himself she scanned the papers and listened to the news and wished that there was some way of finding out if he was back home...

The Colonel, expressing a wish to see him again, had to be told.

'He'll be back. Miss him, do you, Lally?'

Arranging his bedside table just so for the night, she admitted that she did, kissed him fondly and bade him sleep well.

The Colonel, waiting for sleep, thought contentedly that he had no need to worry about Lally's future; Aderik would take care of it. He drifted off gently and died peacefully as he slept.

Somehow or other Eulalia got through the next few days. There was a great deal to do—not least the nephew to notify. There were no other family but old friends had to be told, notices printed in *The Times* and *Telegraph*, the bank manager, his solicitor informed, arrangements for the funeral made. The nephew arrived after two days, a middle-aged kindly man who needed to be housed and fed.

There was no question of Eulalia leaving the house until she had made her own arrangements, he told her. He had a wife and four children who would be coming to England shortly but the house was large enough—he had no intention of turning her out of her home. She thanked him, liking him for his concern, and listened politely to his plans. He was an artist of some repute and was delighted to return to London; the house was large enough to house his family in comfort, and there were attics which could be turned into a studio.

His wife and children arrived in time for the funeral so that Eulalia, opening rooms again, getting ready for their arrival, had little time to grieve. After the funeral he would return to sort out his affairs but his wife and children would remain.

Tom and Pam couldn't have been kinder to her, and the children, although circumstances had subdued them, brought the house alive. Somehow, the funeral which she had been dreading turned into a dignified and serene occasion, with the Colonel's old friends gathered there, making themselves known to Tom and Pam, shaking Eulalia by the hand, asking about her job, telling her in their elderly voices that she was a pretty girl and wasn't it time she married.

However, there were still the nights to get through; there was time to grieve then and wonder what the future held for her. She would have to leave the house, of course, despite Pam's kind insistence that she could stay as long as she wanted to. But at least Jane's future was safe; she was to remain as housekeeper.

The Colonel had left Eulalia his small capital—enough to supplement her wages so that she could rent somewhere. But London was expensive; she would have to find somewhere nearer the hospital and even then she would be eating into her bank balance with little chance of saving. Perhaps she should move away from London, find a job in a small town where she could live cheaply…

She was on compassionate leave from her work but she continued to get up early to go down to the kitchen and help Jane. Still in her dressing gown, her hair hanging tangled down her back, she made tea for them both, laid the breakfast table, fed Dickens and cut the bread while Jane made porridge and collected bacon, eggs and mushrooms.

The new owners of the house enjoyed a good breakfast and Jane, now that she had a generous housekeeping allowance, was happy to cook for hearty eaters. After the skimping and saving she and Eulalia had lived with, it was a treat to use her cooking skills once more. And her future was secure. The one thing which troubled her was Miss Lally, brushing aside her worried questions as to where she was to go and how she would manage, assuring her that she would have no trouble in finding a nice little flat and making lots of friends.

She looked across at Eulalia now, a worried frown on her elderly face. She was beautiful even in that elderly dressing gown with her hair anyhow, but she was pale and too thin. She said, 'Miss Lally…' and was interrupted by the front door knocker being thumped.

'Postman's early,' said Eulalia, and went to open it.

Mr van der Leurs stood there, looking larger than ever in the dim light of the porch lamp.

Eulalia stared up at him, burst into tears and flung herself into his arms. He held her close while she sobbed and snuffled into his cashmere overcoat, unheeding of the early morning wind whistling around them. But when she had no more tears, sucking in her breath like a child, he swept her into the house, shut the door and offered her his handkerchief, still with one arm around her.

'Grandfather died,' said Eulalia into his shoulders. 'I'm sorry I've cried all over you but, you see, I didn't know it was you and I was so glad…'

A muddled speech which Mr van der Leurs received with some satisfaction. 'Tell me about it,

Eulalia.' He propelled her gently into the kitchen, nodded pleasantly to an astonished Jane and sat Eulalia down at the table.

'You don't object to me coming into your kitchen? Eulalia is rather upset. If I might just stay and hear what has happened…'

'It's a blessing that you've come, sir.' Jane was already pouring boiling water into a teapot. 'You just sit there for as long as you like and don't mind me.'

So he pulled out a chair and sat down beside Eulalia. Nothing would ever dim her beauty, he reflected: tousled hair, pink nose, childish sniffs and wrapped in a garment which he supposed was a dressing gown, cut apparently with a knife and fork out of a sack. He asked quietly, 'When did the Colonel die, Eulalia?'

She gave a final sniff and sipped some tea and told him. Her voice was watery but she didn't cry again and he didn't interrupt her. Only when she had finished he said gently, 'Go and get dressed,

Eulalia. Tell Tom that you are going out to have breakfast with me and will be back later.'

When she hesitated he added, 'I'm sure Jane thinks that is a good idea.'

Jane said at once, 'Just what she needs—to get away from us all for a bit, talk about it, make a few plans.'

She gave Mr van der Leurs a sharp look and he smiled. 'Just so, Jane!'

Lally went to the door. She turned round when she reached it. 'You won't go away?'

He got up and opened the door for her. 'No, I won't go away, but don't be long; I'm hungry.'

A remark which made everything seem perfectly normal. Just as it seemed perfectly normal to find the Bentley outside. It was only as they were driving through the early morning traffic that Eulalia asked, 'How long have you been back?'

'I got to Schiphol late last night, went home and got the car and took the late night ferry from Ostend.'

'But you haven't been to bed. You haven't got to go to St Chad's and work…?'

'No. No, I wanted to see you.'

She said faintly, 'But don't you want to get some sleep?'

'Yes, but there are several things I want to do first. We'll go to Brown's and have breakfast.'

It seemed that he was known there. The doorman welcomed them with a cheerful 'Good morning', summoned up someone to park the car and held the door open for them. It was quiet, pleasantly warm inside and for the moment free of people. They sat at a table by a window and an elderly waiter assured them that the porridge was excellent and did they fancy kedgeree?

It wasn't until they were eating toast and marmalade and another pot of coffee had been brought that Mr van der Leurs made any attempt at serious conversation. Only when she asked him how long he would be in London did he tell her that he would be returning to Holland that evening.

When she protested, 'But you can't—you've not been to bed; you must be tired,' he only smiled.

One or two people had come to eat their breakfasts, exchanging polite 'Good mornings' and opening their newspapers. Eulalia leaned across the table, anxious not to be heard.

'Why have you brought me here?'

'To eat breakfast,' he said promptly, and smiled when she said crossly,

'You know that isn't what I mean.'

He said, suddenly serious, 'You know that if I had known about the Colonel I would have come at once?'

'Yes. I don't know quite how I know that, but I do.'

'Good. Eulalia, will you marry me?'

'You asked me once already...'

'In somewhat different circumstances. Your grandfather knew of my intentions and thought it was a good idea.'

She stared at him. 'After I told you I wouldn't...'

'Yes.'

'You mean you were going to ask me again?'

'Of course.' He sounded matter-of-fact. 'Shall we go for a walk and talk about it?'

When she nodded, he added, 'I'll book a table for lunch here. I'll drive you back on my way to the ferry afterwards.'

It was as if he had lifted all her worries and doubts onto his own shoulders, she reflected.

They walked to Hyde Park. There were few people there: dog owners and joggers and a few hardy souls who had braved the chilly November morning. Mr van der Leurs hardly spoke and Eulalia, busy with her chaotic thoughts, hardly noticed. They had walked the length of the Serpentine before he said, 'It is high time that I married, Eulalia, but until I met you I hadn't given it much thought. I need a wife—a professional man does—but I want a friend and a companion too, someone sensible enough to see to my home, to be a hostess to my friends, and cope

with the social side of my life. You know nothing of me but if we marry you may have all the
time you wish for to get to know me.'

Eulalia said gravely, 'But doesn't love come
into it?'

'Later, and only if you wish it…'

'You mean you would be quite happy to have
me as—as a friend until I'd got used to you?'

He hid a smile. 'Very neatly put, Eulalia; that
is just what I mean. And now let us look at the
practical side. You have no home, no money and
no prospects, whereas I can offer you a home,
companionship and a new life.'

He stopped walking and turned her round to face
him. 'I promise you that I will make you happy.'

She looked up into his face. 'I believe you,' she
told him, 'but have you considered that you
might meet a woman you could fall in love with?'

'Yes, I have thought about that too. I am thirty-
eight, my dear; I have had ample time in which
to fall in love a dozen times—and out again.'

'I've never been in love,' she told him. 'Oh, I had teenage crushes on film stars and tennis players but I never met any young men once I'd left school and gone to live with Grandfather. I know almost everyone at St Chad's. But I'm just the canteen lady; besides, I'm twenty-seven.'

Mr van der Leurs restrained himself from gathering her into his arms and hugging her. Instead he said, 'It is obvious to me that we are well suited to each other.'

He took her arm and walked on. Since he was obviously waiting for her to say something, Eulalia said, 'You asked me to marry you. I will.'

And she added, 'And if it doesn't work out you must tell me…'

He stopped once more and this time took her in his arms and kissed her gently, a very light, brief kiss. He said, 'Thank you, Eulalia.'

They walked on again with her arm tucked under his. Presently he said, 'I shall be away for several days after which I can arrange for a day or so to be free. Would you consider marrying by special licence then? I know it is all being arranged in a rush and in other circumstances I wouldn't have suggested it. But I can see no good reason for you to remain any longer than you must at Tom's house. I'm sure he would never suggest that you should leave before you are ready but you can't be feeling too comfortable about it.'

'Well, no, I'm not. Tom is very kind and so is Pam but I'm sure they'll be glad to see me go. I shall miss Jane…'

'Is she also leaving? She may come with you, if you wish.'

'Tom has asked her to stay as housekeeper and she has agreed. She's lived there for years.'

They were retracing their steps. She glanced up at him and saw how tired he was. She said warmly, 'I'll be ready for whatever day you want us to marry. Must I do anything?'

'No… I'll see to everything. If you would give

me the name of your local clergyman and his church, as soon as everything is settled I'll let you know.' He added, 'It will be a very quiet wedding, no bridesmaids and wedding gown, no guests...'

'I wouldn't want that anyway. It would be a sham, wouldn't it? What I mean is we're marrying for...' She sought for words. 'We're not marrying for the usual reasons, are we?'

He reflected that his reasons were the same as any man in love but he could hardly say so. He said merely, 'I believe that we shall be happy together. And now let us go back and have our lunch...'

They had the same table and the same waiter—a dignified man who permitted himself a smile when Mr van der Leurs ordered champagne.

'The lobster Thermidor is to be recommended,' he suggested.

So they ate lobster and drank champagne and talked about this and that—rather like a married couple who were so comfortable in each other's company that there was no need to say much.

Eulalia, spooning Charlotte Russe, felt as though she had known Aderik all her life, which was exactly what he had intended her to think. She liked him and she trusted him and in time she would love him but he would have to have patience...

He drove her back to the house presently and spent ten minutes talking to Tom before leaving. He bade Eulalia goodbye without wasting time and drove away, leaving her feeling lonely and all of a sudden uncertain.

'What you need,' said Pam, 'is a cup of tea. We're delighted for you—Tom and I would never have turned you out, you know, but you're young and have your own life and he seems a very nice man. I'm sure you'll be happy. What shall you wear?'

'Wear?'

'For the wedding, of course.'

'I haven't any clothes—I mean, nothing new and suitable.'

'Well, I don't suppose you'll need to buy

much; your Aderik looks as though he could afford to keep a wife. Tom told me that his uncle has left you a little money. Spend it, dear; he would have wanted you to be a beautiful bride.'

'But it'll be just us…'

'So something simple that you can travel in and wear later on. You go shopping tomorrow; he might be back sooner than you think and you must be ready.'

So the next morning Eulalia went to the bank and, armed with a well-filled purse, went shopping. It wasn't just something in which to be married that she needed; she was woefully short of everything. She went back at the end of the day, laden with plastic bags, and there were still several things which she must have. But she was satisfied with her purchases: a wool coat with a matching crêpe dress in grey and a little hat in velvet to go with them, a jersey dress, and pleated skirt and woolly jumpers and silk blouses, sensible shoes and a pair of high-heeled court shoes to go with the wedding outfit.

Tomorrow she would get a dressing gown and undies from Marks & Spencer. The question of something pretty to wear in case Aderik took her out for an evening was a vexatious one. She had spent a lot of money and there wasn't a great deal left, not sufficient to buy the kind of dress she thought he might like—plain and elegant and a perfect fit. She had seen such a dress but if she bought it it would leave her almost penniless and she had no intention of asking Aderik for money the moment they were married.

This was a tricky problem which was fortunately solved for her. Tom and Pam gave her a cheque for a wedding present, explaining that they had no idea what to give her. 'I'm sure Mr van der Leurs has everything he could possibly want, so spend it on yourself, Lally.'

It was a handsome sum, more than enough to buy the dress, and what was left over she could spend on something for Aderik and tell him it was from Tom and Pam.

Trying the dress on, Eulalia smiled at her reflection in the long mirror. It was exactly right; the colour of old rose, silk crêpe, its simple lines clinging to her splendid shape in all the right places. Perhaps she would never wear it; she had no idea if Aderik had a social life but it would be there, hanging in her wardrobe, just in case...

She displayed it to Tom, Pam and Jane, and packed it away in the big leather suitcase which had belonged to her grandfather. She was quite ready now. Aderik hadn't phoned or written but she hadn't expected him to do so. He was a busy man; he had said that he would let her know when he was coming and it never entered her head to doubt him.

He phoned that evening, matter-of-fact and casual. He would be with her in two days' time and they were to marry on the following morning and travel back to Holland that evening. 'You are well?' he wanted to know. 'No problems?'

'No, none, and I'm quite ready. The Reverend Mr Willis phoned to say he was coming to see me this evening. I don't know why.'

'I asked him to. I don't want you to have any doubts, Eulalia!'

'Well, I haven't, but it will be nice to talk to him. I've known him a long time.'

'I'll see you shortly. I'm not sure what time I'll get to London.'

'I'll be waiting. You're busy? I won't keep you. Goodbye, Aderik.'

She could have wished his goodbye to have been a little less brisk…

Mr Willis came that evening; they had known each other for a number of years and it pleased her that he was going to marry them. 'I would have liked to have met your future husband before the wedding, Lally, but in the circumstances I quite understand that it is not possible. We had a long talk over the phone and I must say I was impressed. You are quite sure, aren't you? He has no doubts but perhaps you have had second thoughts?'

'Me? No, Mr Willis. I think we shall be happy together. Grandfather liked him, you know. And so do I...'

'He will be coming the day after tomorrow? And I understand you will be returning to Holland on the day of the wedding?'

'Yes, it all seems rather a scramble, doesn't it? But he has commitments at the hospital which he must keep and if we don't marry now, in the next day or so, he wouldn't be free for some time. Tom and his wife have been very kind to me but you can understand that I don't want to trespass on their hospitality for longer than I must.'

'Quite so. Both you and Mr van der Leurs are old enough not to do anything impetuous.'

Eulalia agreed, reflecting that buying the rose-pink dress had been impetuous. She didn't think that Mr van der Leurs had ever been impetuous; he would think seriously about something and once he had decided about it he would carry out whatever it was in a calm and unhurried manner…

Mr Willis went away presently after a little talk with Tom, and Eulalia went upstairs and tried on the pink dress once more…

Mr van der Leurs arrived just before midnight. Tom and Pam had become worried when he didn't arrive during the day but Eulalia was undisturbed. 'He said he would be here today, so he'll come. It may be late, though. You won't mind if I stay up and see him? We shan't have time to talk in the morning.'

So she sat in the kitchen with Dickens for company and everyone else went to bed. She had the kettle singing on the Aga and the coffee pot keeping warm. If he was hungry she could make sandwiches or make him an omelette. The house was very quiet and she had curled up in one of the shabby armchairs, allowing her thoughts to wander.

She had lived with the Colonel ever since she had been orphaned, gone to school, lived a quiet life, had friends, gone out and about until her grandfather had lost most of his money. It had been tied up in a foreign bank which had gone bankrupt. He had then been stricken with arthritis of such a crippling nature that there was little to be done for him. It was then that she had found a job. She supposed that if Aderik hadn't wanted to marry her she would have stayed there for the rest of her working life, living in a bedsitter, unwilling to accept Tom's offer of help.

'I'll be a good wife. It will be all right once I know more about him. And we like each other.' She addressed Dickens, sitting in his basket, and he stared at her before closing his eyes and going to sleep again.

He opened them again at the gentle knock on the door and Eulalia went to open it.

Mr van der Leurs came in quietly, dropped a light kiss on her cheek and put down his bag and his overcoat. 'I've kept you from your bed, but I couldn't get away earlier.'

'I wasn't sleepy. Would you like a meal? Come into the kitchen.'

'Coffee would be fine. I won't stay; I just wanted to make sure that everything was all right.'

She was warming milk. 'Have you got somewhere to stay?'

'Brown's. I'll be at the church at eleven o'clock. I've booked a table at Brown's for all of us afterwards. I arranged that with Tom. We can collect your luggage from here later and be in plenty of time for the evening ferry.'

'And when we get to Holland will you be able to have a few days' holiday?'

'A couple of days. You won't see a great deal of me, Eulalia, but as soon as it's possible I'll rearrange my work so that I can be home more often.'

They sat opposite each other at the table, not saying much. She could see that he was tired and she was pleasantly sleepy. Presently he got up, put their mugs tidily in the sink and went with her to the door, put on his coat and picked up his bag. Then he stood for a minute, looking down at her.

He had no doubts about his feelings for her; he had fallen in love with her and he would love her for ever. Now all he needed was patience until she felt the same way.

He bent and kissed her, slowly and gently this time. 'Sleep well, my dear.'

She closed the door behind him and went up to her room and ten minutes later was asleep, her last thoughts happy ones.

She was wakened by Jane with a breakfast tray.

'Brides always have breakfast in bed, Miss Lally, and Mrs Langley says you are to eat everything and no one will disturb you until you're dressed and ready.'

So Eulalia ate her breakfast and then, since it was her wedding day, took great pains with her hair and her face before getting into the dress and coat, relieved to see that they looked just as nice as they had done when she had bought them. And finally, with the little hat crowning her head, she went downstairs.

They were all there, waiting for her, ready to admire her and wish her well, and presently Pam and Jane and the children drove off to the church, leaving Eulalia and Tom to wait until it was time for him to get his own car from the garage and usher her into the back seat.

'Why can't I sit in the front with you?' asked Eulalia.

'Brides always sit in the back, Lally...'

The church was dimly lit, small and ancient and there were flowers. That much she noticed as they reached the porch. She clutched the little bouquet of roses which Aderik had sent that morning and took Tom's arm as they walked down the aisle to where she could see Mr Willis and Aderik's broad back. There was another man there too. The best man, of course. She dismissed him as unimportant and kept her eyes on Aderik. If only he would turn round...

He did, and gave her a warm, encouraging smile which made everything perfectly all right, and since there was nothing of the pomp and ceremony of a traditional wedding to distract her thoughts she listened to every word Mr Willis said and found them reassuring and somehow comforting. She wondered if Aderik was listening too and peeped up into his face. It was calm and thoughtful, and, reassured, she held out her left hand so that he could slip the ring on her finger.

Leaving the church with him, getting into the Bentley with him, she touched the ring with a careful finger, remembering the words of the marriage service. She had made promises which she must keep...

Mr van der Leurs glanced at her serious face. 'The advantage of a quiet wedding is that one really listens, don't you agree?'

'Yes. I—I liked it.'

'And you looked delightful; I am only sorry that we have to hurry away so quickly. You still have to meet my best man—an old friend, Jules der Huizma. We see a good deal of each other. He's married to an English girl—Daisy—you'll meet her later and I hope you'll be friends.'

'Do they live near you? I'm not sure where you do live…'

'Amsterdam but I was born in Friesland and my home is there. When I can arrange some free time I'll take you there to meet my family.'

'It's silly really, isn't it? I mean, we're married and I don't know anything about you.'

'True, but you know me, don't you, Eulalia? And that's important.'

She nodded. 'I feel as if I've known you for a very long time—you know? Like very old friends who don't often meet but know how the other one is feeling.'

Mr van der Leurs knew then that he had his heart's desire, or most of it. Perhaps he wouldn't have to wait too long before Eulalia fell in love with him. He would leave no stone unturned to achieve that.

The luncheon party at Brown's hotel was all that a wedding breakfast should be—champagne, lobster patties, chicken *à la* king, sea bass, salads, red onion tartlets, garlic mushrooms in a cream sauce and then caramelised fruits and ice cream and finally the wedding cake. When it was cut and Eulalia and Aderik's health had been drunk, he made a speech, gave brief thanks and offered regret that they couldn't stay longer and enjoy their friends' company. Then the best man, wishing them well, said he was delighted that he would see more of them in the future.

He seemed nice, thought Eulalia, and wondered why his Daisy wasn't with him—she must remember to ask…

Then it was time to go. She was kissed and hugged and Jane cried a little for they had been through some difficult years together. 'But I'll be back to see you,' said Eulalia. 'Aderik is often over here and I shall come with him.'

She turned and waved to the little group as they drove away. She was leaving a life she knew for an unknown future.

CHAPTER THREE

THEY travelled over to Holland on the catamaran from Harwich and were driving through the outskirts of Amsterdam before midnight. The crossing had been choppy and Eulalia was glad to be on dry land again. The lights of the city were welcoming and she felt a surge of excitement. They hadn't talked much, though Aderik had pointed out the towns they bypassed, but there was no way of seeing them in the dark night.

They had talked about the wedding and he had promised that he would show her as much as possible of Amsterdam before he went back to his usual working day. Now he said, 'I live in the centre of the city; we're coming to a main street—Overtoom—which leads to one of the main squares—Leidseplein—and a little further on I'll turn right onto the Herengracht; that's one of the canals which circle the old part of the city. The house is in a quiet street just off the canal and has been in my family for many years.'

There was plenty to see now. The streets were still bustling with people, cafés were brightly lighted, there were trams and buses and cars. Mr van der Leurs turned into a street running beside a canal bordered by trees and lined with tall narrow houses with steep gables and important-looking front doors.

Eulalia, wide awake by now despite the lateness of the hour, said happily, 'Oh, it's like a painting by Pieter de Hooch…'

'True enough since they might have been painted by him. They knew how to build in those days; all these houses are lived in still.'

He crossed a bridge and turned into a narrow street beside another, smaller canal also lined with trees and a row of gabled houses. The street was short and there was another bridge at its end, too small for cars, spanning yet another canal. It was very quiet, away from the main streets with only the bare trees stirring in the night wind, and as he stopped before the last house Eulalia asked, 'Is this where you live?'

'Yes. Are you very tired? I think that Ko and Katje will be waiting up for us.'

She assured him that she was wide awake as he opened her door and they crossed the street to his front door—a handsome one with an ornate transom above it—and it was now flung open wide as they mounted the two steps from the pavement.

Eulalia hadn't known what to expect. Aderik had scarcely mentioned his home, and she had supposed that it would be a solid, comfortable house, the kind of house she imagined a successful man might live in. But this was something different. She was ushered in and the door was shut behind them before Mr van der Leurs spoke, and that in his own language to the stout, middle-aged man who had admitted them. Then he took her arm. 'Eulalia, this is Ko, who runs our home with his wife. Come and meet everyone.'

She shook hands with Ko who welcomed her in English and then shook hands with his wife, Katje, as stout as her husband, beaming good wishes which Aderik translated. Then there was Mekke, young and buxom, adding her good wishes in hesitant English, and lastly Wim, a small, wizened man 'who has been in the family for as long as I can remember', said Mr van der Leurs. 'He drives the car when I'm not around and sees to the garden.' He looked around him. 'Where is Humbert?'

They had taken the precaution, explained Ko, of putting him in the garden in case *mevrouw* was nervous of dogs.

Aderik looked at her. 'Are you nervous of dogs, Eulalia?'

'No, I like them. May he not come in and meet me? He must be wanting to see you again.'

Ko had understood her and trotted off through a door at the back of the hall.

'*Koffie?*' asked Katje, and trotted after him, taking Mekke and Wim with her.

Mr van der Leurs turned Eulalia round, unbuttoned her coat and cast it on one of the splendid chairs flanking a console table worthy of a museum.

'Then come and meet Humbert.'

He opened a door and led her into a high-ceilinged room with an ornate plaster ceiling, tall narrow windows and a wide fireplace with a great hood above it. There was a splendid fire burning in the fire basket below, adding its light to the sconces on the walls hung with crimson silk. It was a magnificent room and Eulalia stood in the doorway and gaped at it.

But she wasn't allowed to stand and stare. 'This way,' said Aderik, and crossed the floor to another door at the end of the room, opposite the windows. This led to a little railed gallery with steps down to another room. A library, she supposed, for its walls were lined with shelves filled with books and there were small tables and comfortable chairs. But she had no chance to do more than look around her; the room led into a conservatory with a profusion of greenery and elegant cane furniture, and that opened onto the garden, which was narrow and high-walled and surprisingly large.

The dog that rushed to meet them was large too, a great shaggy beast who gave a delighted bark and hurled himself at his master. Then, at a word from Aderik the dog offered a woolly head for her to scratch. Mr van der Leurs switched off the outside lights and closed the door to the garden, then led the way back to the library, through another door in the further wall. Here there was a veritable warren of small rooms until he finally opened the last door which brought them back into the hall.

'Tomorrow,' he assured her, 'you will be given

a leisurely tour of the house. You must be tired; come and have a drink and something to eat and Katje will take you to your room.'

The Stoelklok in the hall chimed the hour as they went back into the drawing room where, on a small table by the fire, Ko was arranging a tray of coffee and a plate of sandwiches. Eulalia, half asleep now but excited too, drank her coffee, and, suddenly discovering that she was hungry, ate several sandwiches.

'What time do you have breakfast?'

'Since I am free tomorrow and we have all day before us, would half past eight suit you?'

She nodded. 'What time do you usually breakfast?'

'Half past seven. I walk to the hospital. If I have a list it starts at half past eight. If you would rather have your breakfast in bed that can easily be arranged.'

'I've only ever had breakfast in bed this morning and I like getting up early…'

'Splendid.' He got up and tugged the bell-pull by the fireplace and when Katje came said, 'Sleep well, my dear. I'll see you at breakfast.'

Eulalia got up, longing now for her bed. She lifted her face for his kiss, quick and light on her cheek, and followed Katje up the oak staircase to the landing above. It was ringed by several doors and another staircase but Katje led her to the front of the house and opened a door with something of a flourish.

The room was already lighted and heavy brocade curtains were drawn across the windows. There was a pale carpet underfoot and a Georgian mahogany and satinwood four-poster flanked by mahogany bedside tables faced the windows between which was a satinwood table with a triple mirror. There was a tapestry-covered stool before it and there were two Georgian armchairs on either side of a mahogany tallboy.

Eulalia caught her breath at the room's beauty as Katje bustled past her and opened the door in a wall, revealing a vast closet; she could see her few clothes hanging forlornly there; someone had unpacked already. Another door led to a bathroom, which Katje crossed to open yet another door, revealing a second room, handsomely furnished but simple.

Katje trotted back, smiling and nodding, and went away. Eulalia lost no time in undressing and bathing before tumbling into bed. The splendid room must be explored thoroughly but not tonight. She was asleep as her head touched the pillow.

She woke as Mekke was drawing back the curtains; the girl wished her a good morning and put a tea tray beside her. She said in English, 'Breakfast soon, *mevrouw*,' and went away. There was an ornate green enamel and gilt clock on the tallboy striking eight o'clock as she drank her tea.

Eulalia nipped from her bed and dressed quickly in a skirt, blouse and sweater, wasted time hanging out of the window in the cold morning air to view the quiet street outside and the canal beyond, then hurried downstairs. The house was alive with cheerful, distant voices and Humbert's deep bark as she reached the hall, uncertain where to go.

Aderik opened a door and then crossed the hall to her, kissed her cheek and wished her a good morning. 'You slept well? Come and have breakfast.'

He ushered her into a small room, very cosy with a small table laid ready for them, and Humbert came prancing to have his head scratched and grin at her.

Eulalia found her voice. 'What a dear little room. Did I see it last night?'

'We came through it but I doubt whether you saw it; you were asleep on your feet, weren't you?'

He smiled at her and pulled out a chair for her before sitting down himself. 'There's tea or coffee; you must let Ko know which you prefer to have.' He added kindly, 'It's all strange, isn't it? But you'll soon find your feet.'

Eulalia said slowly, 'I have the feeling that I shall wake up presently and find that none of this is happening.'

She buttered toast. 'It all happened so quickly…'

'Indeed it did, but now you can have all the time you want to adjust—it is merely that you will be doing it after we are married and not before. I imagine that you would have given your future a good deal of thought if we had waited to marry. You may still do so, Eulalia, and I hope that if you have doubts or problems you will tell me.'

'Yes, I will but I shan't bother you more than I must for you must be very occupied. What else do you do besides operating?'

'I have an outpatients clinic once a week, ward rounds, private patients at my consulting rooms, consultations—and from time to time I go over to St Chad's and occasionally to France or Germany.'

He saw the look on her face. 'But I am almost always free at the weekends and during the week there is the odd hour…'

Waiting for Eulalia in the hall presently, he watched her coming down the stairs. She was wearing a short jacket and no hat; a visit to a dress shop would have to be contrived; a warm winter coat was badly needed and some kind of a hat. It was obvious to him that his dearest Lally was sorely in need of a new wardrobe. He said nothing; he was a man who had learned when to keep silent. In answer to her anxious enquiry he merely assured her that Humbert had had a long walk before breakfast.

'We will come home for lunch and take him for a walk in one of the parks,' he suggested. 'But now I'll show you something of Amsterdam.'

Mr van der Leurs loved his Amsterdam; his roots went deep for a long-ago ancestor had made a fortune in the Indies—a fortune which his descendants had prudently increased—and built himself the patrician house in the heart of the city. The house in which he had been born and grown to manhood. He had left it for long periods—

medical school at Leiden, years at Cambridge, a period of Heidelburg—but now he was firmly established in his profession, making a name for himself, working as a consultant at St Chad's, travelling from time to time to other countries to lecture or examine or attend a consultation.

He wanted Eulalia to love Amsterdam too and, unlike the tours arranged for sightseers, he walked her through the narrow streets away from the usual sights. He showed her hidden canals away from the main *grachten*, old almshouses, houses built out beside the canals so that their back walls hung over the water. He showed her churches, a street market, the flower barges loaded down with colour, gave her coffee in a crowded café where men were playing billiards and the tables were covered with red and white checked cloths, and then wove his way into the elegant streets where the small expensive dress shops were to be found.

Before one of those plate-glass windows he paused.

'The coat draped over that chair…it would suit you admirably and you will need a thick topcoat; it can be so cold here in the winter. Shall we go inside and see if you like it?'

He didn't wait for her to answer but opened the door. Five minutes later Eulalia and he returned to the pavement and this time she was wearing the coat. It was navy blue cashmere and a perfect fit, while on her head was a rakish little beret. The jacket, the friendly saleslady had promised, would be sent to the house.

Eulalia stood in the middle of the pavement, regardless of passers-by. 'Thank you, Aderik,' she said. 'It's the most beautiful thing I've ever possessed.' Her eyes searched his quiet face. 'I—I haven't many clothes and they're not very new.' She looked away for a moment and then gave him a very direct look. 'I hope you're not ashamed of me?'

Mr van der Leurs realised the danger ahead. He said in a matter-of-fact voice, 'You look elegant in anything you wear, my dear, and you are beautiful enough to wear a sack and still draw interested glances. And no, I am not ashamed of you, but I don't want you catching cold when all that are needed are warmer clothes.'

He took her arm and walked on. 'I think that you must get a few things before winter really sets in.'

Put like that, it seemed a sensible suggestion. He glanced down at her face and saw with satisfaction the look of delighted anticipation on it.

They went back to a main street and caught a tram. It was in two sections and both of them were packed. Eulalia stood with his arm around her, loving every minute of it, and then scrambled off when they reached the point where the street intersected the Herengracht. They walked back home from there so that she could find her way back on her own.

They lunched in the small room where they had breakfasted with Humbert sitting between them, happy now that they were home, knowing that presently he would be taken for a walk.

They went to Vondel Park, a long walk which took them past the Rijksmuseum and through a tangle of small streets to the park. Here Humbert raced to and fro while they walked the paths briskly in the teeth of a cold wind.

'Tomorrow we will take the car,' said Mr van der Leurs cheerfully, 'so that you may get a glimpse of Holland. This is not the time of year to see it, of course, but the roads will be empty and we can cover a good deal of ground. You know of St Nikolaas, of course? You must see him with Zwarte Piet riding through the streets. It was once a great day but now we celebrate Christmas much as you do in England. All the same, we exchange small presents and the children have parties.'

He turned her round smartly and started the walk back to the park's gates. 'And after St Nikolaas there will be parties and concerts and the hospital ball and the family coming for Christmas.'

'The family?' asked Eulalia faintly. 'You have a large family?'

'Mother, brother and sisters, nieces and nephews, scattered around the country.'

'You didn't tell me. Do they know you have married me?'

'Yes, and they are delighted. I should have mentioned it; it quite slipped my mind.'

She didn't know whether to laugh or be angry. 'But you should have told me; I might have changed my mind...'

'No, no. You married me, not my family. You'll like them. We don't see much of each other but we like each other.'

'This is a ridiculous conversation,' said Eulalia severely.

He tucked her hand under his arm. 'Yes, isn't it? Let us go home for tea and then I must do some work, much though I regret that. You can make a list of your shopping while I'm doing that and I'll tell you where the best shops are.'

They had tea in the drawing room by the fire—English tea and crumpets.

'Can you get crumpets here?' asked Eulalia, licking a buttery finger.

'There is a shop which sells them, I believe. We don't, as a nation, have afternoon tea, only if we go to a café or tea room.'

'Am I going to find life very different here?'

He thought for a moment. 'No, I think not. You will soon have friends, and there are any number of English living here. I shall take you to the hospital and introduce you to my colleagues there and their wives will invite you for coffee.'

'Oh—but not before I've got some new clothes…'

'No, no. In any case I shall be away for a couple of days next week; I have to go to Rome.'

'Rome? To operate?'

'To examine students. Ko will take care of you.'

He had sounded casual and for some reason

she felt hurt. Surely she could have gone with him or he could have refused to go?

An unreasonable wish, she realised.

He went away to his study presently and she found pencil and paper and made a list of the clothes she might need. The list got longer and longer and finally she became impatient with it and threw it on the table by her chair. What was the use of making a list if she had no idea of how much money she could spend?

She curled up in her chair and went to sleep. It had been an active day and, besides that, her thoughts were in a muddle.

When she awoke Aderik was sitting on a nearby chair with Humbert pressed close to him, reading the list.

He glanced at her and finished his reading. 'You will need more than two evening frocks and a good handful of what my sisters call little dresses. There will be coffee mornings and tea parties. You'll need a raincoat and hat—there's a Burberry shop.'

He took out his pen and added to the list. 'If you'd rather not go alone Ko will go with you, show you where the best shops are and wait while you shop.'

'The best man,' said Eulalia. 'You said he had a wife—Daisy…'

'They had a son two weeks ago. When I get back from Rome we'll go and visit them. I dare say she will go shopping with you if you would like that.'

'If she could spare the time, I would.'

'We will have a day out tomorrow, if you would like that, but will you come to church with me after breakfast?'

'Yes, of course I will. Is it that little church we pass on the way here?'

'Yes; there is service at nine o'clock. I think you may find it not so very different from your own church.'

Eulalia, standing beside him in the ancient, austere little church, reflected that he was quite right. Of course she couldn't understand a word but somehow that didn't matter. And afterwards the *dominee* and several people gathered round to meet her, making her feel instantly at home. That Aderik was well liked and respected among the congregation was obvious, and it struck her anew how little she knew about him.

They went back home for coffee and then, with Humbert on the back seat, set off on their tour.

Mr van der Leurs, a man of many parts, had planned the day carefully. He took the road to Apeldoorn and then by side roads to Zwolle and then north for another twenty miles to Blokzijl, a very small town surrounding a harbour on the inland lakes of the region. It was hardly a tourist centre but the restaurant by the lock was famous for its food. He parked the car and as Eulalia got out she exclaimed, 'Oh, how Dutch! Look at the ducks and that little bridge over the lock.'

She beamed up at him. 'This is really Holland, isn't it?'

'Yes. In the summer there are yachts going to and fro and it can be crowded. Would you like to have lunch here?'

'Oh, yes, please…'

They had a table in a window overlooking the lock in a room half full of people, and Eulalia, with one eye on the scene outside, discovered that she was hungry and ate prawns, grilled sole and Charlotte Russe with a splendid appetite, listening to Aderik's gentle flow of conversation, feeling quietly happy.

They didn't hurry over their meal but presently they drove on, still going north in the direction of Leeuwarden, driving around the lakes and then to Sneek and Bolsward before bypassing Leeuwarden and crossing over to North Holland on the other side of the Ijsselmeer. The dyke road was almost empty of traffic, just over eighteen miles of it, and Mr van der Leurs put his well-shod foot down. Eulalia barely had time to get her bearings before they were on land again, and making for Alkmaar.

They stopped for tea then but they didn't linger over it. 'I'm going to take the coast road as far as Zandvoort. If it's not too dark we'll take a look at the sea.'

The road was a short distance from the sea but very soon he turned off to Egmond aan Zee, a small seaside town, very quiet now that it was winter. He parked the car and together they went down to the beach. It was dusk now, with a grey sky and a rough sea. Eulalia could see the sands stretching away north and south into the distance. 'You could walk for miles,' she said, then added, 'I like it; it's lonely...'

'Now it is. In the summer the beach is packed.'

He took her arm. 'Come, it will be dark very soon. We'll be home in half an hour.'

It was quite dark by the time they got home, to sit by the fire and then eat their supper while

Aderik patiently answered her questions about everything she had seen during the day.

It was lovely, she reflected, sitting there in the beautiful drawing room with Aderik in his chair and Humbert sprawled between them. Despite the grandeur of the room, she felt as though she belonged. She was sleepy too and presently he said, 'Go to bed, my dear; we've had quite a long day.'

'When do you have to go tomorrow?'

'I must leave the house by half past seven.'

'May I come and have breakfast with you? You won't mind if I'm in my dressing gown?'

'That would be delightful. Shall I tell Mekke to call you at seven o'clock?'

'Yes, please, and thank you for a lovely day.' They went to the door together. 'I feel as though I've been here for years and years.' She gave a little laugh, 'That's silly, isn't it? We've only been married a couple of days.'

He smiled and kissed her cheek. 'Sleep well.'

The house was quiet when she went down in

the morning but there were lights on in the dining room and a shaded lamp in the hall. She slid into her chair opposite Aderik, wished him 'Good morning' and told him not to get up. She was wearing the same worthy dressing gown, he saw at once, and her hair was hanging down her back and she was flushed with sleep and very beautiful. He hoped it wouldn't be too long before she fell in love with him...

She asked about his trip and he answered her briefly, promising to phone her that evening. When he got up to go his goodbye was cheerful and brief; nothing of his longing to stay with her showed in his face, which was very calm. She had been happy with him during their two days together: he had seen that in her expressive face—now she would be alone and have time to think about them and realise how happy they had been—and miss him.

It was a gamble, and Mr van der Leurs wasn't a gambling man. But he had faith in his own judgement and a great deal of patience.

He said, 'Ko will take care of you,' and kissed her swiftly, leaving her standing in the hall feeling quite lost.

But not for long. When she came down presently, dressed and ready for the day ahead, Ko was waiting for her. He handed her an envelope and went away to fetch some coffee and she sat down and opened it. There was a great deal of money inside. There was a note too from Aderik. 'Buy as much as you want; if you need more money, ask Ko who will know where to get it.'

She began counting the notes. It seemed like a fortune; she would have to make another list and plan what she could buy. Whatever she did buy would have to be of the best quality. Her coat was of the finest cashmere and she guessed expensive, but Aderik hadn't quibbled over its price. Whatever she bought must match it. She stowed the money away carefully and, seen on her way by a fatherly Ko, left the house.

Years of penny-pinching had taught her to be

a careful shopper and that stood her in good stead now, as she stifled an impulse to enter the first elegant boutique she saw and buy everything which might take her fancy. Instead she sought out some of the bigger stores, inspecting their windows, and presently chose one bearing a resemblance to one of the fashion houses in London and went inside.

She had made a wise choice; the underwear department had everything a well-dressed girl would want. She choked over the prices but even though Aderik was never likely to see her purchases she would feel right. And there was no reason why he shouldn't see a dressing gown—she bought a pink quilted silk garment almost too charming to keep hidden in the bedroom and added it to the pile of silk and lace.

When she had paid for them and asked for them to be delivered to the house, there was still a great deal of money left...

Aderik had told her to buy a Burberry. She

found the shop, bought it and added a matching rain hat, paid for those too and arranged to have them delivered. With the bit firmly between her teeth, she went in search of the boutique where Aderik had bought her coat.

The saleslady recognised her at once. She was alone? she enquired of Eulalia. 'Perhaps *mevrouw* is looking for something special to wear of an evening, ready for the festive season?'

'Well, yes, but first I'd like to see some dresses for the day. Thin wool or jersey?'

'I have just the thing.' The saleslady raised her voice and said something unintelligible to a young girl hovering at the back of the boutique, who sped away and returned presently with several dresses.

'A perfect size twelve,' said the saleslady in her more or less fluent English, 'and a figure to make other women envious, *mevrouw*. Try this jersey dress, such a good colour—we call it mahogany—very simple in cut but elegant enough to wear later in the day.'

An hour later, Eulalia left the boutique, considerably lighter in purse but possessed of a jersey dress, a cashmere twin set, a tweed suit, its skirt short enough to show off her shapely legs, a dark red velvet dress which she was advised could be worn on any occasion after six o'clock, and a pleated skirt, all of which would be delivered to the house. She had tried on several evening gowns too, uncertain which to buy. It was the saleslady who suggested that perhaps she might like to return when it was convenient and bring her husband with her.

Eulalia had agreed although she doubted if he would have the time or the inclination to go with her, but at least she could describe them to him and he could advise her.

She went home for her lunch then; tomorrow was another day and she needed to sit down quietly and check her list and count her money. But first of all after lunch she would put on her coat again and go with Ko and Humbert to Vondel

Park and walk there for an hour while Humbert nosed around happily.

There weren't many people about when they got there for it was cold and the day was closing in but she enjoyed it; Ko had ready answers to all her questions, giving gentle advice, telling her a little about the household's routine.

'And Katje hopes that you will come to the kitchen when you wish; she is anxious that you should know everything. You have only to say when you wish it.'

'I'd like that very much, Ko. When is the best time? I mean, Katje has her work to do.'

'That is thoughtful of you, *mevrouw*. Perhaps in the afternoon after lunch?'

'Tomorrow? You will be there, Ko, to translate…?'

'Naturally, *mevrouw*. Now it is time for us to return.'

The parcels and boxes had been delivered while they had been in the park; Eulalia had her tea by the fire and then went upstairs and un-packed everything and put them in drawers and cupboards. She would go to bed early, she de-cided, and try on everything then.

It was as she was sitting in the drawing room with Humbert pressed up against her that she began to feel lonely. The excitement of shopping had kept her thoughts busy all day but now she wished that Aderik was there. Even if he was working in his study, just to know that he was at home would be nice. They really got on very well, she reflected. Of course they had to get to know each other, and since it seemed that he was away from home a good deal that may take some time. In the meantime she must learn her way around and be the kind of wife he wished for. He would be home again tomorrow—late in the evening, he had said, but she would wait up for him as any good wife would.

He phoned later that evening and she gave a sigh of relief at the sound of his voice.

'You have had a happy day?' he wanted to know.

She told him briefly. It would have been nice to have described her shopping to him in some detail but after a day's work he might not appreciate that. 'I've had a lovely day and Ko took me and Humbert to Vondel Park this afternoon. Have you been busy?'

'Yes. I shall have to stay another day, I'm afraid. I'll ring you tomorrow and let you know at what time I'll be home.'

She tried to keep the disappointment out of her voice. She said, 'Take care, won't you?'

'Yes, and you too. *Tot ziens.*'

It was raining the next morning but that couldn't dampen Eulalia's determination to do some more shopping. In the Burberry and the little hat she went in search of boots and shoes. She had seen what she wanted on the previous day in a shop in the Kalverstraat—boots, soft leather with a sensible heel, and plain court shoes, black, and, since she could afford it, brown as well.

She would need more than these but the boots were expensive and she needed gloves…

Her purchases made, she went into a café and ordered coffee and then walked home, getting lost on the way. Not that she minded; she was bound to miss her way until she had lived in Amsterdam for some time. She had a tongue in her head and everyone seemed to speak English…

After lunch she went to the kitchen and sat down at the big scrubbed table with Ko and Katje. It was a room after her own heart, with a flagstone floor, old-fashioned wooden armchairs on either side of the Aga and a great wooden dresser with shelves loaded with china. There were cupboards too and Katje showed her the pantry, the boot room and the laundry and a narrow staircase behind a door in the wall.

It was a delightful room, and she sat there feeling very much at home, realising that it was her home now.

The afternoon passed quickly, looking into

cupboards with Katje, going round the house once more, examining piles of linen stacked in vast cupboards, being shown where the keys of the house were kept, the wine cellar, the little room where Ko kept the silver locked up.

She had her tea presently, had a long telephone talk with Tom and Pam and then had her dinner. Aderik had said that he would phone and she went back to the drawing room to wait for his call. When he did ring it was almost eleven o'clock and he had little to say, only that he would be home in the late afternoon.

Eulalia put the phone down feeling let down and then she told herself that she was being a fool. Aderik had probably had a hard day; the last thing he wanted to do was to listen to her chatter. And he was coming home tomorrow.

Just before she slept she decided to wear the jersey dress. 'It will really be very nice to see him again,' she muttered sleepily. 'I hope he feels the same about me.'

She woke in the night with the terrible thought that he might not like having her for his wife after all but in the sane light of morning she had forgotten it.

CHAPTER FOUR

IT WAS wet and cold and very windy in the morning. Eulalia was glad that she had done all the shopping she had planned to do and needed little persuasion from Ko to stay indoors. She peered out at the dismal weather and hoped that Aderik would have a good journey home. It was a pity that he hadn't told her if he was likely to arrive earlier. She got into the jersey dress, did her face with extra care and arranged her hair just so before going to the library to wander round its shelves with Humbert for company. She drank her coffee, going every now and then to look out of the window to see if the Bentley was outside.

There was still no sign of it as she ate her lunch and since sitting around waiting was pointless she set off to explore the house again. This time she went to the very top floor and discovered the attics—two rooms under the gabled roof with tiny windows back and front. They were filled with tables and chairs, old pictures, boxes of china and glass and long-forgotten children's toys. There were great leather trunks too; she hauled on their lids and discovered dresses of a bygone age carefully wrapped in tissue paper.

Someone had left a pinny hanging on a door and she put it on for the rooms were dusty and sat down on one of the trunks to examine a large box filled with toys, while Humbert, bored, went to sleep on a pile of rugs.

Mr van der Leurs, coming silently into his house, got no further than the hall before Ko came to meet him, took his coat and his overnight case and offered him coffee or a meal. He wanted neither but took his briefcase to his study and asked, '*Mevrouw* is home? It seems very quiet…'

'She was in the library but I believe she went upstairs.' He added, 'Humbert was with her—devoted he is, already.'

Mr van der Leurs went up the staircase; for such a big man he was light on his feet and quiet. He paused on the landing for his ear had caught a faint sound from somewhere above him. He went on up to the next floor and then opened the small door in a wall which led to the narrow stairs to the attics. It was cold up there, for which reason Eulalia had closed the door at the top of the stairs, and as he opened it Humbert hurled himself at him. Mr van der Leurs stood for a moment, the great dog in his arms, staring over his head at Eulalia, getting to her feet, hampered by the armful of dolls she was holding. She put them down carefully, beaming at him.

'Aderik, you're home…' She took off the pinny. 'I meant to be sitting in the drawing room looking welcoming, only you didn't come so I came up here to pass the time and now I'm a bit dusty.'

Words which brought a gleam to his eye but all he said was, 'How very nice you look; is that a new dress?' He crossed the room and kissed her, a friendly kiss conveying nothing of his feelings. 'How delightful it is to be home again.'

'It's almost tea time but would you like a meal? Did you have a good flight and was the visit to Rome successful?'

'Shall we have tea round the fire and I'll tell you about my trip?'

'Oh, please. I'll just put these dolls back…'

They went back down to the drawing room with Humbert at their heels and found Ko arranging the tea tray before the fire. Since Katje had a poor opinion of the meals Mr van der Leurs was offered when he was away from home, there was a splendid selection of tiny sandwiches, hot crumpets in their lidded dish, currant bread and butter and a Madeira cake—Katje considered that she made the finest Madeira cake in Amsterdam.

Over tea and for an hour or more after, he told her where he had been and why, what he had done and where he had stayed. Listening to his quiet voice gave her the pleasant feeling that they had been married for years, completely at ease with each other and like any other married couple.

'I don't need to go to hospital today,' said Aderik. 'Would you like to meet Daisy? Jules will probably be at home too.'

'Yes, please. Jules looked very nice and I'd like to meet Daisy.'

The der Huizmas lived less than ten minutes' walk away and it was bright and cold. Walking through narrow streets, crossing canals by narrow bridges with Humbert walking sedately beside them, Eulalia asked, 'They don't mind Humbert coming too?'

'No, they have a dog—Bouncer; he and Humbert are the greatest of friends.'

As they mounted the steps to the front door Eulalia saw that the house was very similar to Aderik's but she had no time to look around before the door was opened.

'Joop,' Mr van der Leurs greeted the severe-looking man, who stood aside so that they might enter. 'We're expected? Eulalia, this is Joop who runs the house with Jette, his wife.

'My wife, Joop.'

Eulalia offered a hand and watched the severe elderly face break into a smile before he led the way across the hall to a door which was flung open before they reached it.

The girl who came to meet them was small, with no pretensions to good looks, but her smile was lovely.

Aderik gave her a hug and kissed her soundly. 'Daisy, I've brought Eulalia as I promised.' He turned to greet Jules who had followed his wife.

Daisy took Eulalia's hand. 'You're as beautiful as Aderik said you were. I do hope we shall be friends…'

'I'm sure we shall.' Eulalia was kissed in her turn by Jules who took her coat and hat and urged her into the drawing room. All this while Humbert had been sitting, quivering with impatience, and once in the room he went to greet the rather odd-looking dog who came trotting to meet him. 'Bouncer,' explained Daisy.

Jules added, 'A dog of many ancestors but devoted to all of us as well as Humbert. Come and sit by the fire and tell us what you have been doing since you arrived.'

They talked over their coffee and biscuits and then the two men went to Jules's study and the dogs with them.

'So now shall we go and see Julius? He's three weeks old today. He'll be asleep because I've just fed him. Jules's sister's nanny came to help me for a while but I want to look after him myself—and Jules is marvellous with him.'

She led the way upstairs into a large airy room. There was an elderly woman sitting in a chair knitting who smiled and nodded at them as they went in to bend over the cot.

Julius was sleeping, a miniature of his father, and Daisy said, 'Isn't he gorgeous? We had to call him Julius after Jules's father but it's a nice name, don't you think?'

'Just right for him; he's a lovely boy. You must be so proud of him.'

Eulalia looked at the sleeping baby, thinking she would like one just like him...

Perhaps in a while Aderik would become fond of her—she knew he liked her otherwise he wouldn't have married her, but he treated her as a dear friend and that wasn't the same. He hadn't mentioned love—it was she who had done that and his answer had been almost casual.

Later, on their way back to the house, Eulalia said, 'They're happy, aren't they? Jules and Daisy—how did they meet?'

'Daisy came to Amsterdam to see about some antiques and fell into a canal, and Jules fished her out—they had met in England at her father's antiques shop but I imagine her ducking started the romance.'

'He must love her very dearly—I mean, I don't suppose Daisy looked too glamorous...'

He said evenly, 'I don't imagine that glamour has much to do with falling in love.'

'Well, no, but I should think it might help...'

Next morning they had breakfast together and he left the house directly they had finished, saying he wasn't sure when he would be home. She decided she would go to the shops and get something to do—knitting or tapestry work. Until she knew some people time would hang heavily on her hands. Of course when Aderik had the time he would introduce her to his family and friends...

A question which was partly settled when he got home that evening.

'It will be the feast of St Nikolaas in a day or two,' he told her. 'You will have seen the shops... St Nikolaas comes to the hospital and perhaps you would like to come and see him? It would be a good opportunity for you to meet some of my colleagues there with their wives and children. It's something of an occasion, especially for the children.'

'I'd like that. What time does he come?'

'Eleven o'clock. I'll come and fetch you about half past ten.' He smiled at her. 'I think you'll enjoy it. The day after tomorrow.'

She saw him only briefly the next day for he left the house directly after breakfast. It was evening before he came home and then after dinner he went to his study. When, feeling peevish, she went to wish him goodnight he made no effort to keep her talking.

At breakfast he reminded her to be ready when he came for her.

'You are sure you want me to come?' She

sounded tart and he looked up from the letter he was reading to stare at her.

'Quite sure,' he told her mildly. 'Everyone's looking forward to meeting you.'

Which she decided wasn't a very satisfactory answer.

But she took care to be ready for him and she had taken great pains with her appearance—the new coat, one of the new dresses, the little hat just so on her dark hair, good shoes and handbag. She hoped that she looked exactly as the wife of a respected member of the medical profession should look.

It seemed that she did for when Aderik came into the house he gave her a long, deliberate look and said quietly, 'I'm proud of my wife, Lally.'

She said breathlessly, 'Oh, are you really, Aderik? What a nice thing to say. I'm feeling a bit nervous.'

'No need.' He spoke casually, popped her into the car and drove to the hospital.

Its forecourt was filled with people, mostly children. He parked in the area reserved for the senior consultants and took her into the vast foyer through a side door. There was a crowd round the entrance but there were small groups of people standing and chatting at the back. Eulalia reminded herself that she was no longer the canteen lady and took comfort from Aderik's hand under her elbow and found herself shaking hands with the hospital director and his wife and then a seemingly endless succession of smiling faces and firm handshakes. And Daisy was there with Jules.

'Hello, you do look nice. What did you think of the director and his wife?'

'Friendly; he looks awfully nice and kind and so does his wife.'

'They are. You do know that she is English?' And at Eulalia's surprised look Daisy added, 'Husbands do forget things, don't they? She came over here to nurse, oh, years ago, and they got married and they're devoted to each other. They've got four children, three boys and a girl. Her name's Christina. She's forty-five. She gives lovely dinner parties and we all like her very much.'

She beamed at Eulalia. 'You will be very happy here and Aderik is a dear. We're all so glad that he's found you. You will get asked out a lot, you know.'

The men had joined them and everyone was moving forward to get a good view. St Nikolaas was approaching; they could hear the children shouting and clapping and a moment later Eulalia saw him seated on his white horse, in his bishop's robes, riding into the forecourt with his attendant, Zwarte Piet, running beside him, the sack into which he would put all the naughty children over his shoulder.

The noise was terrific as he got off his horse and stood in the forecourt, an impressive figure who presently addressed his audience in a long speech. Eulalia didn't understand a word but she found it fascinating and when he had finished clapped and cheered as loudly as anyone there.

St Nikolaas came into the foyer then, making his stately way towards the children's wards. He paused to speak to the director, nodded graciously to everyone as he passed and disappeared into one of the lifts with the director and his wife.

Aderik took her arm. 'He will be about half an hour and then he comes back to the courtyard and throws sweets to the children there. We're going to have lunch now—another opportunity for you to get to know everyone.'

He glanced down at her happy face. 'Enjoying it?'

'Oh, yes. Does he go anywhere else?'

'The other hospitals in Amsterdam. Of course there is a St Nikolaas in every town and village. It's a great occasion for the children for he leaves presents for them by the fireplace in their homes and if a grown-up finds a gift by his plate he mustn't ask who it is from but thank St Nikolaas for it. Now if you're ready we'll go and have lunch.'

A buffet had been set up in the consultants' room, a vast apartment furnished solidly with a great deal of brown leather and dark wood. Chairs and tables had been set up and everybody fetched their food and found places to sit with friends.

Mr van der Leurs piled a plate of food for Eulalia, settled her at a table with Daisy, the casualty officer's wife and two younger doctors, promised to be back shortly and went away. The doctors were friendly, only too pleased to tell her about St Nikolaas and Zwarte Piet, and she began to enjoy herself.

Presently they were joined by an older man who introduced himself as Pieter Hirsoff, one of the anaesthetists. He was charming to Eulalia and she responded rather more warmly than she realised. It was pleasant to be chatted up… When he suggested that she might like to see one of the many museums in the city, she agreed readily.

'But not the Rijksmuseum,' she told him. 'Aderik has promised to take me there.'

'I know just the right one for you—a patrician house furnished just as it was when it was first built. It's on one of the *grachten*. Suppose I come for you tomorrow afternoon? I'm sure you will enjoy it.'

He excused himself then and Eulalia joined in the general talk, wondering where Aderik had got to.

He came presently with Jules. They had been up to their wards, they explained, and St Nikolaas was about to leave.

'I'll drive you home,' he told Eulalia, 'but I must come back here for a while.'

Daisy said quickly, 'Come back with us, Eulalia, and have tea. Jules has to come back here and I'd love a gossip. Aderik can fetch you when he's finished here.'

So Eulalia went back to the der Huizmas' and had tea with Daisy and talked about the morning's events. Baby Julius was brought down to be fed and then lay placidly sleeping on Eulalia's lap while they discussed Christmas.

'We go to Jules's family home and so do the rest of his family. It's great fun. I dare say you'll go to Aderik's family. You haven't met them yet?'

'No. There wasn't much time to arrange anything before we married and Aderik doesn't have much free time.'

'Oh, well,' said Daisy comfortably. 'You'll see them all at Christmas. Now you've met everyone at the hospital you'll make lots of friends, but I hope we'll be friends, real friends, you and me.'

It was later that evening as Eulalia and Aderik sat together after dinner that she told him she was going to spend the afternoon with Dr Hirsoff.

Mr van der Leurs had been reading his paper, but now he put it down.

'Which museum are you going to?' He sounded only mildly interested, and when she told him he said, 'Ah, yes, an interesting place. You liked him?'

'Yes. He's very amusing and easy to talk to.'
She looked up sharply. 'You don't like him?'

'My dear girl, what has that to do with it? You
are free to choose your friends and I would
never stand in your way. We are both, I trust,
sensible people, tolerant of each other's tastes
and wishes. I hope you will have a very pleasant afternoon.'

He turned a page and returned to his reading,
leaving her seething although she had no idea
why she was put out. She knew that their marriage wasn't quite like the normal matrimonial
state but surely he should show some interest,
concern even, in the friends she made.

Pieter Hirsoff came for her after lunch and,
since Aderik had phoned to say that he wouldn't
be home until the evening and she had spent the
morning painstakingly discussing household
matters with Katje and Ko, Eulalia was quite
ready to enjoy his company. And he was good
company, guiding her expertly through the mu-

seum and then suggesting that they might have a cup of tea before he drove her home. He took her to a large hotel on the Leidseplein and ordered tea and cakes, and it wasn't until she told him that she would like to go home that he put a hand over hers on the table and smiled across it at her.

'Eulalia, we must meet again. This afternoon has been delightful. We are two lonely people, are we not? My wife doesn't care to live in Amsterdam and Aderik is so engrossed in his work, I doubt if he is home as often as he might be.'

She was too surprised to speak for a moment. She might be twenty-seven years old but there hadn't been much chance to gain worldly experience behind the canteen counter... She quelled a desire to lean over and box his ears; that would never do! He was a colleague of Aderik's. She said in a matter-of-fact voice, 'I'm sorry you're lonely, but I'm not; I'm very happy. Aderik is a marvellous husband and I love living here. I know I shall make lots of friends—his friends too—and I'm sure you'll be one of them. It was kind of you to take me out and I've enjoyed it but now I really must go home.'

'I hope Aderik knows what a treasure he's married.' They were walking to the car. 'I'm a persistent man, Eulalia.'

In the car she said, 'You're being silly now. Aderik and I have only been married for little more than a week; can you not understand that life for us is perfect?'

Which wasn't quite true but surely she would be forgiven for the lie so that she could convince the man? She had thought she liked him, but now she wasn't so sure...

Mr van der Leurs didn't get home until almost dinner time. He came into the drawing room with Humbert, who had gone into the hall to meet him, and bade Eulalia a cheerful hello.

'Did you enjoy your afternoon with Hirsoff?' he wanted to know.

'Since you ask,' said Eulalia tartly, 'I didn't.'

He handed her a drink and asked, still cheerfully, 'Oh? Why not?'

'He got a bit, well, a bit intense…'

'What did you expect? You're a beautiful young woman. It's only logical that he would chat you up.'

She tossed off her sherry. 'What a simply beastly thing to say. And if you knew that he was that kind of a man, why didn't you tell me not to go out with him?'

He had picked up the first of his letters and slit the envelope carefully before he answered.

'When we married—before we married—I told you that you might have all the time you needed to get to know me and settle into your new life. I hope by now that you know that I meant what I said. The fact that we are married and like each other enough to live together doesn't mean that I have any right to dictate to you.'

'You mean that you would never interfere in

anything I might want to do or with the friends that I might make?'

'That is what I mean.'

'You don't mind?' she began angrily, and was interrupted by Ko telling them that dinner was served.

After that there was no chance to go on talking about it. Mr van der Leurs, keeping his thoughts to himself, rambled on about this and that, making it impossible for Eulalia to argue with him. After dinner he told her that he had some phone calls to make and it was an hour or more before he came back to sit by the fire with Humbert at his feet.

Eulalia sat with her newly bought tapestry frame before her, stabbing the needle in and out of the canvas, regardless of the havoc she was making. They were quarrelling, she reflected, or rather she was trying to quarrel; Aderik was being most annoyingly placid. She wondered what she would have to do to ruffle that smooth manner. She couldn't think of anything at the moment so she bade him a chilly goodnight and went to bed, her dignified exit rather spoilt by the kiss he dropped on her cheek as he opened the door for her.

She took a long time to go to sleep. She would have liked someone to confide in but the only person who would have done nicely was Aderik and he, she had to admit, seemed placidly indifferent, rather like an elder brother who didn't want to be bothered but was tolerant of her.

And how absurd, she reflected, half asleep by now, discussing her doubts and worries with the very person who was causing them.

An opinion that was strengthened at breakfast the next morning; Aderik was his usual amiable self but quite clearly he had neither the time nor the inclination to enter into a serious discussion.

He handed her an envelope addressed to them both. 'An invitation to the Christmas ball in a week's time. The invitation was delayed until we returned here but it was taken for granted that we would accept. Send a note to Christina ter Brandt, will you? It's a grand affair...'

'I haven't a dress...'

'Then we will go and buy one. Tomorrow directly after lunch.'

He was looking through his post. 'There are several invitations to dine and here's a letter for you inviting you to have coffee with Christina...'

He added warmly, 'You'll like her: everyone does.' He got up. 'I must go—I've a full day ahead of me so don't expect me until this evening. Why not do some Christmas shopping? Perhaps you can think of something to give Katje—and Mekke is getting engaged. I'll see to Ko.'

'And your family?'

'I'll take a morning off and we'll go shopping together.'

He kissed her cheek swiftly as he went.

Leaving her with a great deal to think about.

His family would come to stay at Christmas, he had told her that, but somehow she hadn't thought any more about it. Now Christmas was less than three weeks away; there would be presents to buy and Katje to consult about meals and rooms. She choked back indignation; he had told her so little…

She sought out Ko. 'Christmas,' she said urgently. 'People will be coming to visit. How long do they stay, Ko? And do we have a tree and holly and give presents?'

He assured her that they did. Christmas, he told her in his careful English, had at one time been a rather solemn occasion, more a church festival, while St Nikolaas had been a more important feast. But Holland had adopted many English customs so that there would be turkey and Christmas pudding, a Christmas tree and decorations and the giving of presents.

'You will wish to consult with Katje, *mevrouw*, and decide on menus and beds for the guests. It will be a relief for *mijnheer* that he has you here to oversee the preparations.'

That evening after dinner, sitting comfortably together, it seemed a good time to her to broach the subject of Christmas.

'There is a great deal I need to know,' she began firmly, 'and I would like you to tell me.'

Mr van der Leurs put down his newspapers, the very picture of an attentive husband. 'Such as?'

'Well, your family. How many are coming to stay and for how long?' A sudden surge of indignation made her voice shrill. 'I know nothing about them.' She added pettishly, 'Probably they won't like me.'

Mr van der Leurs, at his most reasonable, observed, 'How can you say that when you haven't met them?' He saw that she was put out and added in a quite different voice, 'My mother is the kind of mother one hugs and kisses and who offers a cosy shoulder if one wants comforting. My sisters are younger than I am; Marijka is twenty-eight, married and has two children—boys. Lucia is thirty, married, also, with two girls and a boy. Paul is the youngest, twenty-three, in his last year at Leiden. He falls in and out of love so often I've given up trying to remember their names.'

He smiled then. 'Contrary to your expectations, they will like you and you will like them. They will come on Christmas Eve and Katje will be able to advise you as to where they will sleep and so on. I'll get a free morning and we'll go shopping together for presents. I believe that you will find it a Christmas very much like the celebrations in England.'

She had the lowering feeling that she had been making a fuss about nothing but there was still something. 'I have to buy a dress for the ball...'

'Tomorrow afternoon,' he reminded her placidly.

Not a very satisfactory conversation, she reflected; somehow she still felt that she had been making a fuss about nothing.

She went round the house in the morning with Katje, deciding which rooms should be made ready for their guests. There was time enough before Christmas but she wanted everything to be perfect...

Aderik was home punctually for lunch and while she went to put on her outdoor things he took Humbert for a brisk walk.

'And we'll walk too,' he told her. 'It's cold but dry and quicker than taking the car. Where do you want to go first?'

'The boutique where you bought my coat; there were some lovely dresses...'

She spent a blissful hour trying on one gown after another. It was hard to decide and she wanted to wear a dress which Aderik would like. Finally she was left with a choice between a pearl-grey chiffon which fitted perfectly but was perhaps not quite grand enough, and a pale pink taffeta with a square neckline, tiny cap sleeves and a wide skirt. She tried them on again in turn and stood rather shyly while Aderik studied her.

'Have them both,' he decided.

While the saleswoman had gone to supervise their packing, Eulalia said in a whisper, 'But we're only going to one ball...'

'There will be others,' he said. He had got up from the elegant little chair and was wandering around, to stop by a stand upon which a russet velvet dress had been artfully thrown. 'Now, I like that. Will you try it on?'

The saleslady was already at his elbow. 'It is *mevrouw's* size and a perfect colour for her.'

So Eulalia was swept back behind the silk curtains and helped into the velvet dress and, studying her reflection in the long mirror, had to admit that she really looked rather nice in it...

'But when will I wear it?' she wanted to know as they gained the street once more.

'Christmas Day. Now come and help me choose something for my mother...'

* * *

Eulalia had coffee with Christina ter Brandt on the following morning. The ter Brandts lived in a large house in a tree-lined road on the outskirts of den Haag. Aderik had told her that when they were first married Duert ter Brandt had been director of the main hospital there but the last few years had seen him holding the same position in Amsterdam. It was more than half an hour's drive between the two cities but neither of them wished to leave their home in den Haag and Duert enjoyed driving.

Aderik had driven her there, going first to the hospital and coming back for her during the morning, and she had worried that he was wasting his time.

'Not when I'm with you, Lally,' he had told her quietly, 'but it might be a good idea if we were to look around for a car for you. Can you drive?'

'No. We never had a car.'

'Then you shall have lessons. I like to drive you

myself but there may be occasions when that's not possible.'

He had stayed only a few minutes at the house and Christina had told him that she would be going into Amsterdam to have lunch with Duert and would see Eulalia safely home.

Eulalia enjoyed her morning; Christina was the kind of person one could confide in. Not that she did that but she was sure if she ever needed help or advice Christina would give it without fuss. And during the course of the morning she offered tidbits of information about the small everyday problems Eulalia had encountered.

'Of course Aderik will have told you a great deal but men do tend to overlook the small problems—tipping and tram fares and whether to wear a long or short dress; that kind of thing.'

Which reminded Eulalia to ask about the ball.

'Quite an event,' said Christina. 'Long dresses and any jewellery you can lay hands on...' She glanced quickly at Eulalia's hands, bare save for her wedding ring. 'It's all rather dignified and stately but great fun. You have met quite a few of the wives at the hospital? You'll meet a lot more but you'll only need to smile and murmur. You're rather a nine days' wonder, you know. Aderik's family are coming for Christmas? They always do; they're all delightful so don't worry about meeting them.'

Christina poured more coffee. 'What do you think of the shops in Amsterdam?' she asked, and the conversation moved on.

She drove Eulalia back presently. 'I don't suppose Aderik will be back for lunch? It's been fun meeting you; you must come again and perhaps we can meet Daisy one morning here and have coffee?'

She drove away and Eulalia, warmed by her friendliness, had her lunch and then sat down to write Christmas cards and make a painstaking list of people for whom she would need to buy presents.

It seemed a good idea to go shopping the next day. Aderik would be away until mid-afternoon but if she had an early lunch she would have time to do at least some of her shopping—the children's presents, perhaps.

She went down to breakfast ready to tell him, to find that he had left the house in the early hours of the morning. An emergency, Ko told her, but he hoped to be home during the afternoon, probably around four o'clock.

So after lunch she set out with her list and a nicely filled purse. She felt at home in the city now although she was familiar only with the main streets. That morning, while she had been in the kitchen, she had told Katje that she was going shopping; it was surprising how well they understood each other as long as they kept their conversation to basics. Mekke had been there too, helping them out when they reached an impasse. Her English was only a smattering but she was quick to understand and quick to learn.

When Eulalia had mentioned that she wanted to buy toys for the children she had told Eulalia where to go: a large store near the Central Station. *Mevrouw* must take a tram to the station and then walk; the shop was close by and she would find all the toys she could wish for there. She had even drawn a map to make finding it easy.

Eulalia clutched it as she walked to the Leidsestraat and got into a tram. It took her a few minutes to find the street Mekke had written down and when she reached the shop it was packed with people so that it took her longer than she expected to find just what she wanted.

The final purchases made, she glanced at her watch. Aderik would be home in a short while and she wanted to be there. She joined the surge of people leaving the store and started walking briskly, confident of her direction.

She had been walking for several minutes when it dawned on her that she was in a street she didn't know. Somehow she must have missed a turning. Not a serious matter, she told herself, and turned to walk back the way she had come. It was a narrow street and there were few people in it and no shops.

She stopped the first person coming towards her and asked the way; her Dutch was negligible but 'Central Station' and an arm waved enquiringly should be enough. It seemed that it wasn't; she tried two more people and was about to try again when the faint drizzle became a downpour. She was brushed aside; no one wanted to hang around answering questions in such weather…

There was no shelter and she could hardly knock on a door, while to try and find her way on her own was a waste of time… She wasn't the Colonel's granddaughter for nothing; she walked on until she saw a telephone box.

It took time to find the right coins and decipher the instructions, and, although there was no one

about, the street outside, its lights almost ob-
scured by the rain, looked menacing. She dialled
and heard Aderik's voice.

'It's me. I'm lost and it's raining…'

He was reassuringly calm. 'Do you know the
name of the street?'

'No, it's dark and—and empty.'

Mr van der Leurs, stifling a panic which astonished him, became all at once briskly reassuring.

'You're in a phone box? Tell me the number
on the dial. Did you tell anyone where you
were going?'

'Yes, Mekke. To a big toy shop near the station…'

'Stay where you are, Lally. I'll be with you
very shortly.'

'I'm sorry to be a nuisance…' Her voice had a
decided squeak.

'You've been very sensible, my dear; just stay
where you are.'

* * *

Mr van der Leurs went into the hall and found
Ko. 'Ask Mekke to come here, will you?'

When she came, he asked, 'Mekke, this shop
you suggested *mevrouw* should visit—which
street?' And when she told him he went on, 'And
is there another entrance?'

'Yes, *mijnheer*, at the back of the shop.' She put
her hand to her mouth. '*Mevrouw* has lost herself?'

'Only temporarily. Do you know the street? Is
there a phone box in it?'

'Yes. Turn left as you leave the shop.'

Mr van der Leurs nodded, whistled to Humbert
and went out to his car. The streets were jammed
with traffic but he knew a number of back ways…

He slid to a halt by the phone box and got out,
opened its door and took Eulalia in his arms.

'My poor dear, you're wet and cold…'

'I was getting frightened too,' muttered Eulalia
into his shoulder. 'I don't know why I got lost…'

'There was another entrance at the back of the
shop—a natural mistake.'

He gathered up her parcels and shoved her gently into the car. 'Humbert's in the back.'

The car was warm and comfortable and Humbert pushed his woolly head against her shoulder. Eulalia supposed it was relief which made her want to cry. She sniffed away the tears and Aderik, without looking at her, said cheerfully, 'Dry clothes and tea and then you can show me what you have bought.'

CHAPTER FIVE

BACK at the house, Aderik pulled off her wet gloves, took off her coat and gave it to a hovering Ko and tossed her hat into a chair while Katje and Mekke, both talking at once, urged her to get into something warm.

'I'm only a bit wet,' protested Eulalia, and shivered.

'You appear half drowned. Go and get into something dry; your feet are sopping. And don't be long; I want my tea.'

So she went up to her room with an emotional Mekke in attendance, declaring in a mixture of English and Dutch that it was all her fault; she should never have told *mevrouw* to go to that shop. If *mevrouw* caught cold she would never forgive herself...

Ten minutes later Eulalia went back downstairs. Mekke had taken away her wet shoes and damp skirt and she had got into a jersey dress, brushed her hair and done her face, none the worse for her soaking. She had been frightened; she hoped that Aderik hadn't noticed that...

But of course he had.

He was standing with his back to the fire, his hands in his pockets and Humbert lolling beside him, while Ko arranged the tea things on a small round table between the two armchairs drawn up to the blaze.

Eulalia heaved a sigh of contentment; it was lovely to be home and she told him so. 'I'll be more careful next time,' she told him earnestly.

'It's easy to get lost,' he said easily, 'but you will soon find your way around. I must arrange for you to have lessons in Dutch so that you can ask the way. There are parts of Amsterdam where

English might not be understood. I'm sorry that
you got so wet…'

She had hoped that he might have said more
than that; that it had been sensible of her to
phone, a word of praise for her good sense and
lack of panic, but he began a casual conversation
about Christmas, dismissing the whole thing as
trivial, reflected Eulalia pettishly.

Mr van der Leurs, watching her expressive face
from under his eyelashes, thought his own
thoughts and presently asked her if she would
like to go shopping with him in the morning.
'I'm free until two o'clock; we might get the
family presents bought. You found what you
wanted for the children?'

'Yes. I hope they'll do; I mean, I haven't seen the
children yet, have I? I don't know what they like.'

He didn't answer that but asked abruptly, 'Are
you happy, Eulalia?'

She was too surprised to say anything for a moment. She put down the toasted teacake she was

on the point of eating and licked a buttery finger. She said composedly, 'Yes, I am happy. Why do you ask, Aderik?'

'When I asked you to marry me I promised that you could have all the time you needed to get to know me and adjust to a new way of life. Ours was hardly a traditional marriage, was it? There should be time to reflect on the future together before becoming man and wife and I gave you no time for that. You may have regrets or doubts. And I think that you like me well enough to tell me if that is the case?'

She said thoughtfully, 'I don't think I ever had any doubts or regrets. Perhaps I should have thought about it more…but I feel at home here although it's much grander than I had expected. And I miss Grandfather…but we get on well together, don't we? And in a little while, as soon as I've learnt to speak Dutch and become the kind of wife you want…'

'You are the kind of wife I want, Lally. Stay

just as you are. Learn to speak Dutch by all means, but don't change.'

He got up and pulled her gently to her feet. 'And now that you are quite certain that you are happy here with me I think that it is time we became engaged!'

He had put his arm around her shoulders and she stared up at him.

'Engaged? But we are married!'

'So now we will be engaged as well.'

He took a little box out of his pocket and opened it. There was a ring inside—diamonds in an old-fashioned gold setting. 'My grandmother's ring—I had it altered to fit your finger.'

He picked up her hand and slipped it above her wedding ring and, before she could speak, bent and kissed her. A gentle, slow kiss which left her with a surge of delight, so unexpected that she lost her breath.

'Oh,' said Eulalia, and kissed him back.

Mr van der Leurs' arms tightened around her

for a moment, then he let her go. 'Sealed with a kiss,' he said lightly. 'Now tell me, have you any ideas about these presents?'

Eulalia sat down again, feeling vaguely disappointed, telling herself that she had no reason to be; hadn't Aderik just given her a most beautiful ring? And the kiss—she refused to think about that for the moment. It hadn't been like the other brief kisses he had given her—brief tokens of affection; it had left her feeling unsettled.

Mr van der Leurs, sitting in his chair, Humbert's great head resting on his knee, watched her face, and because he loved her so deeply he guessed her thoughts and was satisfied. A little more time and a lot more patience, he reflected.

They went shopping in the morning and Eulalia, at Aderik's quiet direction, bought silk scarves, exquisite handbags, gloves as supple as velvet, earrings for his mother, thin gold bangles for his sisters, books for his brother, before having a cup of coffee while they decided what to get Katje, Ko and Mekke. Soft fleece-lined slippers for Ko, whose elderly feet would be glad of them at the end of the day, and silk-lined gloves for Katje. As for Mekke—a quilted dressing gown in one of the bright colours she loved...

They went home, well pleased with their purchases, and after an early lunch Aderik left for the hospital, leaving Eulalia sitting at the little writing desk in the small sitting room, carefully writing Christmas cards from the list he had given her. It was a long list, prudently updated from year to year so that all she had to do was copy names and addresses. Tomorrow, she decided, she would buy presents to send to England; the cards she had already sent. And she still had to find a present for Aderik.

The days passed surprisingly quickly, with last-minute presents to buy, Humbert to take for walks, and rather anxious preparations for the ball, now only a day or two away. And Aderik was seldom home before the early evening. So it was all the more delightful when she went down to breakfast on the morning before the day of the ball to be told that he was free until the afternoon and would she like to see more of Amsterdam?

'Not a museum; we'll save those for when we have hours of leisure. Suppose we just walk round some of the older streets? Most of them have little antique or book shops and the small houses are worth seeing.'

It was a day for walking: a cold blue sky, frost underfoot and the city bustling with preparations for Christmas. But the small streets to which Aderik led the way were quiet. The small gabled houses had their doors shut, spotless curtains shrouding their gleaming windows. From time to time they met a housewife, basket on arm, going to the shops, and exchanged good mornings, and they stopped frequently to look in the shop windows.

Eulalia found them fascinating—book shops

galore and antiques shops, some with their goods spread out on the narrow pavement. Aderik bought her a small china bowl, patterned in the lavender colour, which was the first Delftware. It had a small chip and a hairline crack yet was none the less expensive, but since she didn't know the price and Mr van der Leurs paid without comment she accepted it with delight.

It was as they were on their way back, going down a narrow lane with a few shops and rather shabby cottages, that Eulalia stopped suddenly before a window. There was a kitten sitting in a cage there, a puny little creature with huge eyes. Attached to the cage was a card with 'Goedkoop' written on it.

Eulalia tugged at Aderik's sleeve. 'How could anyone be so callous?' she demanded. 'Writing "cheap" on that card, just as though the little creature is fit for nothing. And supposing no one wants him? He'll just die.'

Mr van der Leurs looked down at her furious

face, flushed with rage, her eyes flashing. She looked so beautiful he could hardly keep his hands off her. He said, 'We want him; he's just the companion Humbert will enjoy.'

The smile she gave him was his reward. 'You'll buy him? I'll look after him; he won't be a nuisance...'

He opened the door and its old-fashioned bell tinkled rustily and an elderly man came through the curtain at the back of the shop. Eulalia couldn't understand what was said; the man sounded apologetic and had a great deal to say while Aderik listened silently. Presently he handed the man some notes and the kitten was fetched out from the window, removed from his cage and transferred to the inside of Aderik's topcoat, and they were ushered out of the shop with some ceremony.

'Oh, Aderik, thank you. I'm sure he'll grow into a splendid cat. That horrible man...'

'He had a so-called pet shop there but is moving away. He sold the animals he had, and the shop, but this small creature for some reason wasn't sold, so he put it in the window as a last hope before being drowned.'

He added, 'Don't be sad; he's going to be our family pet and he's too small to remember his unhappy start. We'll cut through here; there's a shop in the next street where we can buy him a basket and anything else he needs.'

Eulalia was struggling not to cry. She had no reason to do so; the kitten was safe, Aderik had dealt with the unhappy little episode with instant calm; for some reason she realised that was why she wanted to cry. And that was absurd. He was a man of unfailing kindness. She might not know him very well yet but of that she was sure. And she trusted him…

Back at the house the kitten was laid on a clean towel, given warm milk and gently examined. He was in poor shape but Aderik thought that with good food and tender loving care he had a good chance of growing into a handsome cat. All the same, he would take him to the vet when he got home later in the day. So the kitten was settled in the basket Aderik had bought for him, lined with paper and a blanket, before the warm hearth. Humbert, at first doubtful and puzzled, came and sat beside him and presently, to their delight, the kitten crawled out of his basket and curled up between Humbert's paws.

Mr van der Leurs was late home; the bone marrow transplant he had done that afternoon had had unexpected complications and he would have to go back to the hospital later on. Nevertheless he took the kitten to the vet before he sat down to his dinner.

'Nothing wrong with him,' he assured Eulalia. 'He's had his injections and a thorough overhaul; all he needs now is feeding up and warmth.'

'And to be loved,' said Eulalia. 'And he must have a name—an important one to make up for an unhappy start. Something grand...'

They were sitting in the drawing room with

Humbert lying on Aderik's feet and the kitten half buried against the great dog's furry chest.

'Ferdinand,' said Eulalia, 'and we can call him Ferdie. Oh, Aderik, I'm so glad you saved him.'

'He's made himself at home; I hear that Katje is mincing chicken and keeping milk warm on the Aga and obviously Humbert is pleased to have him.'

He got up carefully from his chair. 'I have to go back to the hospital. I'll say goodnight, Lally, and see you at breakfast. Ko will see to Humbert and Ferdie.'

He brushed her cheek with a quick kiss, a brief salute which left her feeling lonely. 'How can I possibly feel lonely?' asked Lally of her two companions.

And indeed she had no leisure to feel lonely; the next day was spent attending to Ferdie's needs, taking Humbert for a walk and then getting down to the serious business of dressing for the ball. She had decided on the pink taffeta and when she was finally dressed she had to admit that she really looked rather nice. She had taken pains with her face and her hair, and the fine cashmere shawl which she had had the forethought to buy made a warm and dramatic wrap against the cold night. There remained nothing for her to do but go down to the drawing room and wait for Aderik.

He was late, she thought worriedly; perhaps there had been an emergency which would hold him up for hours, and they might have to miss the first part of the evening, even the whole evening. She sat there trying not to fidget in case it creased her dress, thinking how much she had been looking forward to the ball. She hadn't been to a dance for a long time; she had always refused invitations to the annual dance at St Chad's; she couldn't afford a dress for one thing and for another she had been afraid that no one would dance with the canteen lady… But now she had the right clothes and a husband to partner her, and she very much wanted to dance with Aderik.

She glanced at the clock once more, heard voices in the hall and just had time to compose her features into serenity as the door opened and Aderik came in.

Annoyingly unhurried. Eulalia bit back wifely admonishments to hurry up and change, smiled as though time were of no importance at all, and said, 'Hello, Aderik. Would you like a drink before you change?'

He had shut the door and was leaning against it looking at her.

'Eulalia, you leave me speechless. I was prepared to see an impatient virago hissing at me to hurry up and change and did I know the time? Instead of which I find a charming vision in pink offering me a drink!'

He crossed the room and pulled her to her feet. 'You look beautiful and that is a most becoming gown.' He held her away so that he could study her at his leisure. 'My enchanting wife,' he said quietly and then dropped her hands and added briskly, 'Give me fifteen minutes,' and was gone…

He was as good as his word and returned the epitome of a well-dressed man with time on his hands.

Eulalia said uncertainly, 'You won't leave me alone, will you?'

He hid a smile. 'No, Lally, although I think that you will have more partners than you will be able to cope with. Shall we go?' When she got up and picked up her wrap, he added, 'Just a moment,' and took a long box from an inner pocket. 'I have never given you a wedding present, have I?'

He took the double row of pearls from the box and fastened it round her neck and bent to kiss her. 'I wanted you to feel free, Lally…'

She knew what he meant; he had wanted her to marry him without any strings attached. She said simply, 'Thank you, Aderik. You are so good to me and thank you for that too.'

She turned to look in the gilt wood mirror above a wall table and put a hand up to touch the pearls. 'They're very beautiful.'

The ball was being held in the assembly hall of the hospital and the place was packed. The ter Brandts were standing by the doors, shaking hands and exchanging greetings as the guests arrived. Christina kissed Eulalia and said warmly, 'You look lovely; Aderik must be so proud of you. He'll be lucky to have more than two or three dances with you. Daisy and Jules are here already; it's quite a crush but you'll find them when the dancing stops.'

She turned to Aderik and Duert kissed Eulalia's cheek. 'I shall want a dance with you later,' he told her.

They joined the dancers then—they were playing a waltz and she gave herself up to the delight of dancing; it was as though she and Aderik had danced together all their lives and for a moment she was oblivious of anything but his arm around her and her feet following his of their own volition. But presently he said, 'There are many people here whom you met when you came to see St Nikolaas, but you won't remember all of them.'

He was greeting other couples as they danced and she hastened to nod and smile too, feeling shy. When the dance ended and a rather pompous man and his wife approached them, Aderik said, 'You remember Professor Keesman, Eulalia? And his wife?'

Eulalia murmured politely and Mevrouw Keesman said kindly, 'You have met so many new faces, it must be difficult for you. You must come and visit me soon—after Christmas perhaps? I should like that.'

Eulalia barely had time to thank her before Professor Keesman danced her off into a slow foxtrot. He was a short stout man and she discovered quickly that he was self-important too, impressing upon her the high rank of his position in the hospital. She listened politely, making appropriate replies when necessary, thinking that Aderik never boasted about his work, nor did Duert, and she suspected that they were just as important as the professor. She hoped that Aderik wasn't a close friend of the Kessmans; she much preferred Duert and Jules.

But if she didn't much care for the professor there were any number of guests there who professed to be close friends of Aderik. She didn't lack for partners and from time to time she would find him at her elbow introducing her to one or other of them and claiming her for a dance.

They had supper with Daisy and Jules and half a dozen couples who obviously knew each other well and Eulalia got up from the supper table with enough invitations to fill her days for weeks to come. And when they went back into the ballroom Aderik whisked her onto the dance floor.

'Now we can dance together until the end,' he told her. 'My duty dances are done and you have had partners tumbling over each other to get at you; now we can behave like an old married couple and dance together.'

'Oh, yes, please,' said Eulalia. 'I feel so comfortable with you and I've run out of polite small talk!'

'But you are enjoying yourself? You have been much admired.'

'I've had a lovely time. I did my best to behave like a consultant's wife. I hope I didn't let you down. I mean, not remembering names and not being amusing or witty.'

She felt his arm tightening round her. 'My dear Eulalia, do not, I beg you, try to change in any way. You are delightful as you are, restful and soft-voiced and with the happy knack of knowing when to talk and when to keep silent.'

In other words, reflected Eulalia, dull. It was a depressing thought but if that was what he wanted in a wife then she would endeavour to be just that.

Somehow—she wasn't sure why—the pleasures

and the excitement of the evening had evaporated. Which was absurd. She had had partners and compliments and there had been young women of her own age only too ready to make friends.

She watched Daisy and Jules dancing together and had a sudden pang of envy. And the ter Brandts, no longer in their first youth but obviously devoted... But of course they're in love, thought Eulalia wistfully.

The ball wound to a close and the guests began a leisurely departure, calling goodnights, stopping to chat with friends before going out into the cold night.

Back home, Aderik said, 'Shall we have a warm drink before we go to bed? Katje will have left something ready for us.'

The kitchen was cosy and neither Humbert nor Ferdie did more than open an eye as they went in.

'Hot cocoa?' suggested Eulalia, and fetched mugs from the dresser and the plate of sandwiches she had asked Katje to make. 'Supper seems a long while ago,' she observed. 'I asked Katje to make them with ham and there's cold chicken…'

'Bless you for being a thoughtful housewife,' said Aderik, and took a huge mouthful before sitting down at the table opposite her. 'What a pleasant way to end the evening.'

He smiled at her. 'And you looked lovely, Lally. I am a very much envied man.'

She thanked him gravely. 'I've never been to a grand ball before; it was exciting.' She put down her mug. 'I think I'll go to bed.'

He got up and went to the door with her. 'Shall we go and buy the Christmas tree in the morning? I've private patients to see in the afternoon but otherwise I'm free.'

'Oh, yes—and a little one for Katje and Ko and Mekke?'

'Of course. We'll go into the country. Goodnight, Lally.'

She went to her bed feeling deprived. A goodnight kiss would have set the seal on the evening.

* * *

It was mid-morning before they set out. Humbert had to have his walk, Ferdie needed to be fed and brushed and made much of and Katje needed to discuss what they should have for dinner that evening...

'We'll have lunch out,' said Aderik. 'I need to be back soon after one o'clock.'

He drove out of Amsterdam and took the road to Hilversum, some twenty miles away, and then turned off the main road into a narrow country lane running between flat fields. There was wooded country ahead of them and when they reached it there was a small village, well hidden from the road.

Aderik parked by a small farm at the edge of the village and they got out and walked across the yard and round the back to find an old man surrounded by Christmas trees in all shapes and sizes. He shouted a greeting to Mr van der Leurs and came to shake hands and then shake Eulalia's. He had a great deal to say, too, in his gruff old voice, nodding and shaking his head and then leading them among the trees. They chose a splendid one for the house and a small one for the kitchen and Eulalia wandered off, leaving Aderik to pay and talk to the man. Presently he joined her.

'The trees will be delivered in two days' time. They'll be in tubs and his son will bring them and carry them into the house.'

'He'll need a tip? How much do I give him?'

'Ten guilden—I've paid for transport...'

'And a cup of coffee,' said Eulalia, very much the housewife.

Christmas was near now; Eulalia's days were filled wrapping presents, deciding on menus with Katje—a hilarious business with Ko patiently translating the more complicated remarks, although he was quick to tell her that her Dutch was improving each day. And then there was Humbert needing a walk even on a wet day, and Ferdie, still puny but beginning to look more like a kitten should.

There was Daisy to visit too and new-found friends phoning and Christina coming for coffee. Life was perfect, Eulalia told herself, ignoring the thought that all the same there was something not quite right... Perhaps it was because she didn't see much of Aderik: an hour or two in the evening, a brief half-hour at breakfast.

It was Christina who told her that he had agreed to take several teaching rounds. 'And I can't think why,' she added. 'Duert told him that they could be fitted in after the New Year so that he could be free instead of staying at the hospital in the afternoons.' She didn't say any more because she had seen the look on Eulalia's face. Had they quarrelled? she wondered, and dismissed the idea as absurd, sorry that she had said it.

Eulalia tried to forget about it. Aderik had his reasons for wanting to fill his days with work and when he was home he was as kind and friendly to her as he always was—only he was so seldom home…

She told herself she was worrying about nothing and flung herself into the final arrangements for the arrival of their guests.

Paul arrived first on the day before Christmas Eve, breezing into the house just before lunch, clapping Ko on the back, kissing Katje and Mekke, hugging Eulalia, demanding to know where Aderik was. He was almost as tall as his brother and very like him in looks, bubbling over with good spirits.

'I'm not supposed to be here until this evening, am I? But I couldn't wait to meet you. You're even more beautiful than Aderik said. Am I in my usual room? Is lunch at half-past twelve? I'm famished.'

Eulalia liked him. When he was ten years older he would be just like Aderik.

'How much longer will you be in Leiden?' she asked over lunch.

'Another year. I'm qualified but I want to specialise. I'd like to go to England, work in a hospital there and get some experience. Of course I'll never reach the heights Aderik has—he's top of the tree. I only hope I'll be half as good.'

They took Humbert for his walk presently and soon after they got back Aderik came home in time to greet the rest of his family, his arm around Eulalia as he introduced her to his mother who was unexpectedly small and plump with grey hair pulled severely back from a kind face, to his sisters, tall and good-looking, and their husbands and five children.

'It is too bad,' said Mevrouw van der Leurs, 'that you should have to meet all of us at once, and more so since Aderik tells me that you have no family. But we welcome you most warmly, Eulalia, and hope that you will adopt us as your own.' Eulalia, hugged and kissed and made much of, reflected that this was going to be a wonderful Christmas.

And so it was. The children were small enough

to believe in Father Christmas and the old house rang with their small voices, and after tea everyone helped decorate the tree, glittering with baubles and with a magnificent fairy doll topping it, and then they all went to the kitchen while Katje and Ko decorated the smaller tree with the children's help.

Since it was Christmas time dinner was served earlier than usual so that the children could stay up for it, and Eulalia, looking round the table, thought how marvellous it was to belong to such a happy family. She caught Aderik's eye, sitting at the head of the table, and beamed at him, and he smiled back briefly as he turned to speak to his mother.

For a moment she felt chilled. But it was impossible to be downcast; Paul took all her attention and when they got up from the table she went upstairs with Lucia and Marijka and helped them put the children to bed. Afterwards they sat and talked over coffee and the delicious little biscuits Katje had made.

Mevrouw van der Leurs declared that she was tired and would go to bed—the signal for everyone else to do the same. Eulalia, kissed goodnight and complimented on the delicious dinner and pleasant evening, was left alone with Aderik, and she asked anxiously, 'Was it really all right? Just as you wanted it?'

'It was perfect, Eulalia.'

'Oh, good. Your mother is a darling, isn't she? And your sisters and brother and the children.' She gave a small sigh. 'They're all so happy.'

'Does that mean that you're not, Lally?'

'No, no, of course not. I was only thinking that I've missed so much. Although Grandfather and Jane were always so good to me.' She added sharply, 'I'm not whinging…'

'No, no; I never thought you were. I'm glad that you do like the family—your family as well as mine.'

'Well, I think it's very nice of them not to mind that you married me in such a hurry.' She got up. 'I'm going to bed. Will you make sure that Ferdie's comfortable when you take Humbert to his basket?'

He went to open the door for her. 'I'm going to the hospital in the morning but I'll be back for lunch. Would you like to go to the midnight service at the English church?'

'Oh, yes. Daisy told me about it. All of us?'

'No, just you and me. The family will go to morning service which will give us the chance to put the presents round the tree.'

Her eyes shone. 'It's like a fairy-tale Christmas,' she told him, and leaned up to kiss his cheek.

Mr van der Leurs went back to his chair. In fairy tales, he reflected, the prince always won the hand of the princess. Which was what he intended to do.

Christmas Eve passed in a happy bustle: last-minute talks with Katje, walking with Paul and the children and Humbert while Lucia and Marijka saw to the children's presents, Ferdie to feed and play with, chatting to her mother-in-law over coffee and then Aderik coming home and the house alive with children's voices. But all five had an early supper and were put to bed and dinner was a leisurely meal with easy talk and a lot of laughter.

The house was quiet when Aderik and Eulalia went out to the car. It was bitterly cold but there were stars and half a moon casting its icy light. The city was thronged with people and although the shops were long since shut their lighted windows rivalled the lighted Christmas trees in the squares. The church was in a small enclosure off Kalverstraat, surrounded by a ring of old houses, and was already almost full. Eulalia saw Christina and Duert ter Brandt almost at once, and then Daisy and Jules.

There was a Christmas tree and holly and flowers and a choir. It was all so English and she felt tears prick her eyelids. The congregation burst into the opening carol and after a moment she joined in.

It took some time to leave the church once the service was over, there were so many people to exchange good wishes with. The streets were quieter now and the shop windows dark, but as they reached the house she could see a glimmer of light through the transom over the door and inside it was warm and very welcoming.

'Coffee in the kitchen if you would like it,' she told Aderik, and went ahead of him to fill the mugs and get it ready.

He came into the kitchen presently, took the mugs from her and set them on the table. 'Happy Christmas, Lally. I'm cheating and giving you your present while we are alone together.'

It was earrings, gold and diamonds with a pearl drop.

Eulalia looked up at him. 'Aderik—they are so very beautiful; I've never seen anything as lovely. Thank you over and over again; you are so good and kind to me.' She kissed his cheek. 'May I try them on now?'

She slipped the hooks into her ears and went to look in the small looking-glass by the dresser, turning this way and that, her eyes shining.

It would be so easy, he thought, watching her, to play on her happiness and gratitude, but that wasn't what he wanted. If she came to love him it had to be of her own free will…

'Could I wear them to breakfast?'

He laughed then. 'Well, perhaps lunch would be a better choice. What dress are you wearing?'

'The russet velvet you chose.' She beamed at him as she sat down to drink her coffee. 'I'm so happy I could burst,' she told him, and presently, her coffee drunk, she wished him goodnight and went off to bed, still wearing the earrings.

Everyone was up early in the morning and breakfast was eaten to a chorus of seasonal greetings. The children could hardly eat for excitement and were presently borne away to church, leaving Aderik and Eulalia to collect up the presents and arrange them round the tree. They went to the kitchen first with the gifts for Katje, Ko and Mekke. Wim was there too, shaking hands and having a great deal to say to Eulalia, who didn't understand a word but made up for that by smiling a lot and looking interested. He was profuse in his thanks for the box of cigars and the envelope Mr van der Leurs gave him and went to sit by the Aga, for he was to spend the day there, joining in the festivities.

The presents arranged, Aderik took Humbert for his walk and Eulalia fetched Ferdie to sit in his little basket in the drawing room and then everyone was back from church to drink coffee.

Eulalia had decided that their traditional Christmas dinner should be eaten at midday so that the children could join in before the presents were handed out. She had taken great pains with the table and on her way upstairs went to check that everything was just so. It looked magnificent with the white damask cloth, silver and sparkling glass. She had made a centrepiece with holly and Christmas roses and gold ribbon and the napkins were tied with red ribbon. She went to her room then, got into the russet velvet dress and fastened the pearls, put in the earrings and went back to the drawing room.

That night curled up in her bed, waiting for sleep, Eulalia re-lived the day. It was one that she would always remember for it had been perfect. Christmas dinner had been a success; the turkey, the Christmas pudding, the mince pies, the wines and champagne had all been praised. And as for the presents, everyone had declared that everything they had received was exactly what they wanted.

She closed her eyes to shut out the thought that she and Aderik had had no time to be together, had exchanged barely a dozen words. If she hadn't been so sleepy she might have worried about that.

In Holland, she had discovered, there wasn't a Boxing Day but a second Christmas Day, only the names were different. The day was spent looking at presents again, going for a walk, playing games with the children and having friends in for drinks in the evening. She spent it being a good hostess, making endless light conversation with Aderik's friends and their wives, trying out her fragmented Dutch on her sisters-in-law, being gently teased by Paul and all the while wishing for Aderik's company.

Everyone went home the next day and the house was suddenly quiet, for Aderik had gone to the hospital in the early morning. She had slipped down to sit with him while he had breakfast but there was no time for a leisurely talk.

'I shall probably be late home,' he'd told her, getting up to leave. 'I've a list this morning and a clinic in the afternoon.'

She mooned around the house with Humbert padding beside her and Ferdie tucked under one arm. 'I do miss them all,' she told Humbert, and then changed that to, 'I do miss Aderik.'

It was nearly lunchtime when Ko came looking for her. He looked so anxious that she said, 'Ko, what's the matter? Are you ill?'

'*Mevrouw*, there has been a message from the hospital, from the director. There has been an explosion in one of the theatres and I am to tell you not to worry.'

'Aderik,' said Eulalia—and, thrusting Ferdie at Ko, flew past him and into the hall, to drag on an elderly mac she kept for the garden. She dashed out of the house, racing along the narrow streets, oblivious of the cold rain and the slippery cobbles. If he's hurt, I'll die, she told herself. She said loudly, 'Oh, Aderik, I love you. I think I always have and now perhaps it's too late and how silly of me not to know.'

She glared at a solitary woman standing in her way and pushed past her. She was sopping wet and bedraggled when she reached the hospital and the porter on duty gave her a shocked look and started towards her, but she flew past him and belted up the stairs to the theatre unit. She had to pause then for the place was thronged with firemen and police and porters carrying away equipment. They were all too busy to notice her. She edged her way through, looking for someone who would know where Aderik was. He might even now be being treated for injuries—or worse, said a small voice in the back of her head.

She was dodging in and out of the various side rooms and then saw the main theatre at the end of the corridor, its doors off the hinges, everything in it twisted and smashed. She slithered to a halt and almost fell over when Aderik said from somewhere behind her, 'My dear, you shouldn't be here.'

She turned on him. 'Why didn't you tell me, phone me? You must have known I'd be half out of my mind. You could have been hurt—killed. I'm your wife.' She burst into tears. 'And it doesn't matter to you but I love you and I really will not go on like this.'

She stopped, aware that she was babbling, that that was the last thing she had meant to say to him. She wiped a hand across a tear-stained cheek and muttered, 'I didn't mean to say that.' She gave a great sniff and said in a small polite voice, 'I hope you haven't been hurt.'

Mr van der Leurs wasted a moment or so looking at her—hair in wet streamers, a tear-smeared face, in an old mac fit for the refuse bin and thin slippers squelching water. And so beautiful…!

He removed the wet garment from her and took her into his arms.

'My darling,' he said gently, 'why do you suppose I married you?'

'You wanted a wife.' She sniffed again.

'Indeed I did. You. I fell in love with you the moment I set eyes on you at St Chad's. I knew that you didn't love me, but I was sure that if I had patience you would find that you love me too.'

'You never said…' mumbled Eulalia.

'I cherished the thought that you would discover it without any help from me.'

His arms tightened around her. 'I'm going to kiss you,' he said.

'Oh, yes, please,' said Eulalia.

They stood there, the chaos around them forgotten, watched by silent onlookers: firemen, doctors, police and porters and the odd nurse, all of them enjoying the sight of two people in love.

THE
DOCTOR'S
GIRL

CHAPTER ONE

MISS MIMI CATTELL gave a low, dramatic moan followed by a few sobbing breaths, but when these had no effect upon the girl standing by the bed she sat up against her pillows, threw one of them at her and screeched, 'Well, don't just stand there, you little fool, phone Dr Gregg this instant. He must come and see me at once. I'm ill; I've hardly slept all night...' She paused to sneeze.

The girl by the bed, a small mousy person, very neat and with a rather plain face enlivened by a pair of vivid green eyes, picked up the pillow.

'Should you first of all try a hot lemon drink and some aspirin?' she suggested in a sensible voice. 'A cold in the head always makes one feel poorly. A day in bed, perhaps?'

The young woman in the bed had flung herself back onto her pillows again. 'Just do as I say for once. I don't pay you to make stupid suggestions. Get out and phone Dr Gregg; he's to come at once.' She moaned again. 'How can I possibly go to the Sinclairs' party this evening…?'

Dr Gregg's receptionist laughed down the phone. 'He's got three more private patients to see and then a clinic at the hospital, and it isn't Dr Gregg—he's gone off for a week's golf—it's his partner. I'll give him the message and you'd better say he'll come as soon as he can. She's not really ill, is she?'

'I don't think so. A nasty head cold…'

The receptionist laughed. 'I don't know why you stay with her.'

Loveday put down the phone. She wondered that too, quite often, but it was a case of beggars not being choosers, wasn't it? She had to have a roof over her head, she had to eat and she had to earn money so that she could save for a problematical future. And that meant another year or two working as Mimi Cattell's secretary—a misleading title if ever there was one, for she almost never sent letters, even when Loveday wrote them for her.

That didn't mean that Loveday had nothing to do. Her days were kept nicely busy—the care of Mimi's clothes took up a great deal of time, for what was the point of having a personal maid when Loveday had nothing else to do? Nothing except being at her beck and call each and every day, and if she came home later from a party at night as well.

Loveday, with only an elderly aunt living in a Dartmoor village whom she had never met, made the best of it. She was twenty-four, heart-whole and healthy, and perhaps one day a man would come along and sweep her off her feet. Common sense told her that this was unlikely to be the case, but a girl had to have her dreams...

She went back to the bedroom and found Mimi threshing about in her outsize bed, shouting at the unfortunate housemaid who had brought her breakfast tray.

Loveday prudently took the tray from the girl, who looked as if she was on the point of dropping it, nodded to her to slip away and said bracingly, 'The doctor will come as soon as he can. He has one or two patients to see first.' She made no mention of the clinic. 'If I fetch you a pot of China tea—weak with lemon—it may help you to feel well enough to have a bath and put on a fresh nightie before he comes.'

Mimi brightened. Her life was spent in making herself attractive to men, and perhaps she would feel strong enough to do her face. She said rudely, 'Get the tea, then, and make sure that the lemon's cut wafer-thin...'

Loveday went down to the basement, where Mrs Branch and the housemaid lived their lives. She took the tray with her and, being a practical girl, ate the fingers of toast on it and accepted the mug of tea Mrs Branch offered her. She should have had her breakfast with Mrs Branch and Ellie, but there wasn't much hope of getting it now. Getting Miss Cattell ready for the doctor would take quite a time. She ate the rest of the toast, sliced the lemon and bore a tray, daintily arranged, back upstairs.

Mimi Cattell, a spoilt beauty of society, prepared for the doctor's visit with the same care she took when getting ready for an evening party. 'And you can make the bed while I'm bathing—put some fresh pillowcases on, and don't dawdle...'

It was almost lunchtime by the time she was once more in her bed, carefully made up, wearing a gossamer nightgown, the fairytale effect rather marred by her sniffs. To blow her nose would make it red.

To Loveday's enquiry as to what she would like for lunch she said ill-temperedly that she had no appetite; she would eat something after he had visited her. 'And you'd better wait too; I want you here when he's examining me.'

'I'll fetch a jug of lemonade,' said Loveday, and sped down to the kitchen.

While Ellie obligingly squeezed lemons, she gobbled down soup and a roll; she was going to need all her patience, and the lowering feeling that the doctor might not come for hours was depressing.

She bore the lemonade back upstairs and presently took it down again; it wasn't sweet enough! She was kept occupied after that— opening the heavy curtains a little, then closing them again, longing to open a window and let a little London air into the room when Mimi sprayed herself once more with Chanel No 5. By now Mimi's temper, never long off the boil, was showing signs of erupting. 'He has no right to leave me in such distress,' she fumed. 'I need immediate attention. By the time he gets here I shall have probably got pneumonia. Find my smelling salts and give me the mirror from the dressing table.'

It was getting on for two o'clock when Loveday suggested that a little light lunch might make her employer feel better.

'Rubbish,' snarled Mimi. 'I won't eat a thing until he's examined me. I suppose you want a meal—well, you'll just have to wait.' Her high-pitched voice rose to a screech. 'I don't pay you to sit around and stuff yourself at my expense, you greedy little...'

The door opened by Ellie, and after one look the screech became a soft, patient voice. 'Doctor—at last...'

Mimi put up a hand to rearrange the cunning little curl over one ear to better advantage. 'I don't think we've met,' she purred. To Loveday, she said, 'Pull the curtains and get a chair for the doctor, and then go and stand by the window.' The commands were uttered in a very different voice.

The doctor opened the curtains before Loveday

could get to them and pulled up a chair. 'I must introduce myself, Miss Cattell. I am Dr Gregg's partner and for the moment looking after his patients while he is away.'

Mimi said in a wispy voice, 'I thought you would never come. I am rather delicate, you know, and my health often gives cause for concern. My chest…'

She pushed back the bedspread and put a hand on her heart. It was annoying that he had turned away.

'Could we have the window open?' he asked Loveday.

A man after her own heart, thought Loveday, opening both windows despite Mimi's distressed cry. She would suffer for it later, but now a few lungfuls of London air would be heaven.

From where she stood she had a splendid view of the doctor. He was a tall man, with broad shoulders and fair hair flecked with grey. He was good-looking too, with a rather thin mouth and a splendid nose upon which were perched a pair of spectacles. A pity she couldn't see the colour of his eyes…

Miss Cattell's voice, sharp with impatience, brought her to the bedside. 'Are you deaf?' A remark hastily covered by a fit of sneezing, necessitating the use of a handkerchief and nose-blowing.

The doctor waited patiently until Mimi had resumed her look of patient suffering. He said mildly, 'If you will sit up, I'll listen to your chest.'

He had a deep voice, pleasantly impersonal, and he appeared quite unimpressed by Mimi's charms, ignoring her fluttering breaths and sighs, staring at the wall behind the bed while he used his stethoscope.

'Clear as a bell,' he told her. 'A head cold. I suggest aspirin, hot drinks and some brisk walks in the fresh air—you are quite near Hyde Park, are you not? Eat whatever you fancy and don't drink any alcohol.'

Mimi stared up at him. 'But I'm not well—I'm delicate; I might catch a chill...'

'You have a head cold,' he told her gravely, and Loveday had to admire his bedside manner. 'But you are a healthy woman with a sound pair of lungs. You will be perfectly fit in a couple of days—less, if you do as I suggest.'

Mimi said rudely, 'I'll decide that for myself. When will Dr Gregg be back? I don't know your name...?'

'Andrew Fforde.' He held out a large hand. 'I'm sure you will let me know if you don't make a full recovery.'

Mimi didn't answer. Loveday went to the door with him and said gravely, 'Thank you for coming, Doctor.' She went downstairs with him, along the hall and opened the front door. As he offered a hand and bade her a grave good afternoon she was able to see that his eyes were blue.

A sensible girl, she went first down to the

kitchen, where Mrs Branch and Ellie were sitting over a pot of strong tea.

'I've saved you a bite of lunch,' said Mrs Branch, and pushed a mug of tea across the table. 'That weren't Dr Gregg. Ellie says 'e looked a bit of all right?'

'Dr Gregg's partner, and he was nice. Miss Cattell has a head cold.' Mrs Branch handed Loveday a cheese sandwich. 'You'll need that. Well, will she be going out this evening?'

'I should think so,' said Loveday in a cheese-thickened voice.

Miss Cattell was in a splendid rage; the doctor was a fool and she would speak to Dr Gregg about him the moment he was back. 'The man must be struck off,' declared Mimi. 'Does he realise that I am a private patient? And you standing there with the windows wide open, not caring if I live or die.'

Mimi tossed a few pillows around. 'Where have you been? You can get me a gin and tonic…'

'Doctor said no alcohol.'

'You'll do as I say! Make it a large one, and tell Cook to make me an omelette and a salad. I want it now. I shall rest and you can get everything ready for this evening.'

'You are going to the party, Miss Cattell?'

'Of course I am. I don't intend to disappoint my friends. I dare say I'll be home early. I'll ring for you if I am.'

Another half an hour went by while Mimi was rearranged in her bed, offered her omelette and given a second gin and tonic. She finally settled, the windows shut and curtains drawn, for a nap. Loveday, free at last, went to her room on the floor above, kicked off her shoes and got onto the bed. Some days were worse than others…

Miss Cattell was still asleep and snoring when Loveday crept into her room an hour later. In the kitchen once again, for yet another cup of tea, she thankfully accepted Mrs Branch's offer of a casserole kept hot in the oven for her supper.

Mimi wouldn't leave the house before half past eight or nine o'clock, and there would be no chance to sit down to her supper before then.

Later, offering more China tea and wafer-thin bread and butter, Loveday was ordered to display a selection of the dresses Miss Cattell intended to wear. She meant to outshine everyone there and, her cold forgotten, she spent a long time deciding. After the lengthy ritual of bathing, making up her face and doing her hair, and finally being zipped into a flimsy dress which Loveday considered quite indecent, she changed her mind. The flimsy dress was thrown in a heap onto the floor and a striking scarlet outfit was decided upon, which meant that shoes and handbag had to be changed too—and while Loveday was doing that Ellie was ordered to bring another gin and tonic.

Loveday, escorting Mimi to a taxi, had the nasty feeling that the night was going to prove worse than the day had been. She was right; she was wakened at two in the morning by the noisy return of Miss Cattell and several of her friends, who thankfully didn't stay, but that meant she had to go downstairs and help Mimi up to her room.

This was no easy task; Mimi was too drunk to help herself, so that hoisting her upstairs and into her room was a herculean task. Loveday was strong even though she was small, but by the time she had rolled the lady onto her bed she decided that enough was enough. She removed Mimi's shoes, covered her with a light blanket and went back to her own bed.

In a few hours she had to get up again and face Miss Cattell's rage at discovering herself still clad in scarlet crêpe, lying untidily under a blanket. Even worse than that, her dress was torn and stained; Loveday had never heard such language…

When Miss Cattell was once more bathed, her make-up removed, and attired in a satin and lace confection, she declared that she would remain in bed for the rest of the day. 'My cold is still very heavy.' She snorted. 'Cold indeed. That man had no idea of what he was talking about.'

Loveday allowed her thoughts to dwell upon him, and not for the first time. She had liked him. If she were ever ill she would like him to look after her. She frowned. In different surroundings, of course, and in a nightie like Miss Cattell wore. She dismissed the thought as absurd, but as the day wore on it was somehow restful to think about him while Mimi's cross voice went on and on.

On her half-day off, she went to the public library and searched the papers and magazines, looking for jobs. 'Computer skills…knowledge of a foreign language useful…anyone under the age of twenty-five need not apply…kitchen hands willing to work late nights…' A splendid selection, but none of them would do. And they all ended with references required. She didn't think that Miss Cattell would give her a reference, not one which would secure her a job.

As it turned out she was quite right.

It was Mrs Branch who told her that Miss Cattell had quarrelled with the man she had decided she would marry, which was possibly an excuse for her to be even more bad-tempered than usual, and solace herself by filling the house with her friends, going on a shopping spree and staying up until all hours.

It was on the morning after one of Mimi's parties that a bouquet of roses was delivered. They must be arranged at once, she ordered, and there was a particularly lovely vase into which they must go.

Loveday arranged them carefully under her employer's eye and bore them from room to room while Mimi decided where they should go. It was unfortunate that, getting impatient, she turned sharply and knocked the vase and flowers out of Loveday's hands.

'My vase,' she screamed. 'It was worth hundreds of pounds. You careless fool; you'll pay for this...'

She gave Loveday a whack over one eye. 'You're fired. Get out now before I send for the police!'

'If anyone sends for the police it will be myself,' said Loveday. 'It was your fault that I dropped the vase and you hit me. I shall leave at once and you can do what you like.' She added, 'I'm very glad to be going.'

Miss Cattell went an ugly red. 'You'll not get a reference from me.'

'I don't expect one. Just a week's wages in lieu of notice.'

Loveday left Mimi standing there and went to her room and packed her few things tidily before going down to the kitchen.

'I'm leaving,' she told Mrs Branch. 'I shall miss you and Ellie; you've both been very kind to me.'

'You're going to have a black eye,' said Mrs Branch. 'Sit down for a second and drink a cup of tea. Where will you go?'

'I don't know…'

'Well, if it's any help, I've a sister who lives

near Victoria Park—Spring Blossom Road—she has rooms. Wait a tick while I write 'er a line. She'll put you up while you sort yerself out.'

Ellie hadn't said a word, but she cut ham sandwiches and wrapped them neatly and gave them to Loveday. It was a kind gesture which almost melted Loveday's icy calm.

She left the house shortly afterwards; she had her week's wages as well as what was owed her in her purse, but she tried not to think of the things Mimi had said to her. It would have been a pleasure to have torn up the money and thrown it at her, but she was going to need every penny of it.

Mrs Branch's sister, Mrs Slade, lived a far cry from Miss Cattell's fashionable house. Loveday, with Mrs Branch's directions written on the back of an envelope, made her way there, lugging her case and shoulder bag. It was a long journey, but there was a lull in the traffic before the lunch hour and the bus queues were short.

Spring Blossom Road couldn't have seen a

spring blossom for many years; it was a short, dingy street with small brick houses on either side of it. But it was tolerably quiet and most of the windows had cheerful curtains. It was a relief to find that Mrs Slade had the same kind, cheerful face as her sister. She read Mrs Branch's note and bade Loveday go in.

"Appens I've got the basement vacant,' she told Loveday. 'It's a bit dark, but it's clean.' She smiled suddenly. 'Not what you've been used to, from what I've 'eard. Take it for a week while you find yourself a job. It'll be rent in advance but I'll not overcharge you.'

Then she led the way to the back of the house, told Loveday to sit down at the kitchen table and offered tea.

'That's a nasty eye you've got there—Miss Cattell had one of her tantrums? My sister only stays until Ellie gets married. I don't 'old with these idle folk with nothing better to do than get nasty.'

The tea was hot and strong and sweet and

Loveday felt better. This was something which had been bound to happen sooner or later; she should count herself lucky that Mrs Branch had been so kind and helpful and that she had two weeks' wages in her bag.

She went with Mrs Slade to inspect the basement presently. It was a small room below street level, so that the only view was of feet passing the window. But there was a divan bed, a table, two chairs and a shabby armchair by a small electric fire. There was a sink in one corner, and a small door which led to the neglected strip of back garden. 'Outside lav. Nice and handy for you,' explained Mrs Slade. "Ere's a key, and you'd better pop down to the corner and get yourself some food. There is a gas ring by the sink so you can cook if you want to.'

So Loveday went to the small shops at the end of the road and bought eggs, butter, tea and a bottle of milk. She still had the ham sandwiches, which would do very nicely for her supper…

She was a sensible girl, and now that her boats were burnt behind her she was cheerfully optimistic. Loveday ate her sandwiches, drank more tea and contrived to wash at the sink before venturing cautiously into the back garden to find the loo. And then, tired by such an eventful day, she got onto the divan and went to sleep. Her eye was painful but there was no mirror for her to inspect it, only her tiny powder compact which was quite inadequate.

It was raining in the morning and there was the first chill of autumn in the air. Loveday boiled an egg, counted her money and sat down to plan her day. She couldn't remember her mother and father, who had both died in a rail crash while she was still a toddler, but the stern aunt who had brought her up had instilled in her a number of useful adages. 'Strike while the iron is hot' was one of them, and Loveday intended to do just that.

She would visit the nearest job centre, the public library, and make a round of the adverts in the small shop windows. That would be a start. But before she did, she allowed her thoughts to wander a little. Miss Cattell would certainly insist on Dr Gregg visiting her, and if she did that she would be able to complain about Dr Fforde. She hoped she would not; they hadn't exchanged two words and yet she had the firm feeling that she knew him well.

Her eye was painful and almost closed, and, had she but known it, was the reason why the job centre lady wasn't very helpful. She had to admit that it looked rather awful when she caught sight of it in a passing shop window. Tomorrow, if it wasn't better, she would go to the nearest hospital and get something for it. Next she applied for a job as a waitress in a large, noisy café and was told to stop wasting time by the proprietor.

'Oo's going to order from a girl with an eye like that? Been in a fight, 'ave yer?'

The next morning she caught a bus to the hospital, a mile away. It was a vast Victorian building, its Casualty already overflowing. Since Loveday's eye wasn't an urgent case, she was told to sit on one of the crowded benches and wait.

The benches didn't seem any less crowded; rather the opposite. At midday she got a cup of coffee and a roll from the canteen and then settled down to wait again. She was still waiting when Fforde, on his way to take a clinic in outpatients, took a short cut there through Casualty. He was late and he hardly noticed the sea of faces looking hopefully at him. He was almost by the end doors when he caught sight of Loveday, or rather he caught sight of the black eye, now a rainbow of colours and swollen shut.

It was the mouse-like girl who had been with that abominable Miss Cattell. Why was she here in the East end of London with an eye like that? He had felt an instant and quite unexpected liking for her when he had seen her, and now he realised that he was glad to have found her again, even if the circumstances were peculiar. He must find out about her… He was through the doors by now and encircled by his clerk, his houseman and Sister, already touchy because he was late.

Of course by the time he had finished his clinic the Casualty benches were almost empty and there was no sign of her. Impelled by some feeling he didn't examine, he went to Casualty and asked to see the cases for the day. 'A young lady with a black eye,' he told the receptionist. 'Have you her address? She is concerned with one of my patients.'

The receptionist was helpful; she liked him, for he was polite and friendly and good-looking. 'Miss Loveday West, unemployed, gave an address in Spring Blossom Road. That's turn left from here and half a mile down the road. Had her eye treated; no need to return.'

He thanked her nicely, then got into his car and drove back to his consulting room. He had two patients to see and he was already late…

There was no reason why he should feel this

urge to see her again; he had smiled briefly, they had exchanged goodbyes on the doorstep and that was all. But if the opportunity should occur…

Which it did, and far more rapidly than he anticipated.

Waiting for him when he reached his rooms on the following morning was Miss Priss, his receptionist-secretary. She was a thin lady of middle years, with a wispy voice and a tendency to crack her knuckles when agitated, but nevertheless she was his mainstay and prop. Even in her agitation she remembered to wish him a good morning before explaining that she had had bad news; she needed to go home at once—her mother had been taken ill and there was no one else…

Dr Fforde waited until she had drawn breath. 'Of course you must go at once. Take a taxi and stay as long as you wish to. Dr Gregg will be back today, and I'm not busy. We shall manage very well. Have you sufficient money? Is there anyone you wish to telephone?'

'Yes, thank you, and there is nobody to phone.'

'Then get a taxi and I'll ask Mrs Betts to bring you a cup of tea.'

Mrs Betts, who kept the various consulting rooms clean, was like a sparrow, small and perky and pleased to take a small part in any dramatic event.

Miss Priss, fortified by what Mrs Betts called her 'special brew', was seen on her way, and then Dr Fforde sat down at his desk and phoned the first agency in the phone book. Someone would come, but not until the afternoon. It was fortunate that Mr Jackson, in the rooms above him, was away for the day and his secretary agreed to take Miss Priss's place for the morning...

The girl from the agency was young, pretty and inefficient. By the end of the next day Dr Fforde, a man with a well-controlled temper, was having difficulty in holding it in check. He let himself into his small mews house, tucked away behind a terrace of grand Georgian mansions, and went from the narrow hall into the kitchen, where his housekeeper, Mrs Duckett, was standing at the table making pastry.

She took a look at his tired face. 'A nice cuppa is what you're needing, sir. Just you go along to your study and I'll bring it in two shakes of a lamb's tail. Have you had a busy day?'

He told her about Miss Priss. 'Then you'll have to find someone as good as her to take her pace,' said Mrs Duckett.

He went to his study, lifted Mrs Duckett's elderly cat off his chair and sat down with her on his knee. He had letters to write, a mass of paperwork, patients' notes to read, and the outline of a lecture he was to give during the following week to prepare. He loved his work, and with Miss Priss to see to his consulting room and remind him of his daily appointments he enjoyed it. But not, he thought savagely, if he had to endure her replacement—the thought of another day of her silly giggle and lack of common sense wouldn't bear contemplating.

Something had to be done, and even while he thought that he knew the answer.

Loveday had gone back from the hospital knowing that it wasn't much use looking for work until her eye looked more normal. It would take a few days, the casualty officer had told her, but her eye hadn't been damaged. She should bathe it frequently and come back if it didn't improve within a day or so.

So she had gone back to the basement room with a tin of beans for lunch and the local paper someone had left on the bench beside her. It was a bit late for lunch, so she'd had an early tea with the beans and gone to bed.

A persistent faint mewing had woken her during the small hours, and when she'd opened the door into the garden a very small, thin cat had slunk in, to crouch in a corner. Loveday had shut the door, offered milk, and watched the small creature gulp it down, so she'd crumbled bread into more milk and watched that disappear too. It was a miserable specimen of a cat, with bedraggled fur and bones and it had been terrified. She'd got back into bed, and presently the little beast had crept onto the old quilt and gone to sleep.

'So now I've got a cat,' Loveday had said, and went off to sleep too.

This morning her eye was better. It was still hideously discoloured but at least she could open it a little. She dressed while she talked soothingly to the cat and presently, leaving it once more crouching there in the corner, she went to ask Mrs Slade if she knew if it belonged to anybody.

'Bless you, no, my dear. People who had it went away and left it behind.'

'Then would you mind very much if I had it? When I find work and perhaps have to leave here, I could take it with me.'

'And why not? No one else will be bothered with the little creature. Yer eye is better.'

'I went to the hospital. They said it would be fine in another day or two.'

Mrs Slade looked her up and down. 'Got enough to eat?'

'Oh, yes,' said Loveday. 'I'm just going to the shops now.'

She bought milk and bread and more beans, and a tin of rice pudding because the cat so obviously needed nourishing, plus cat food and a bag of apples going cheap. Several people stopped to say what a nasty eye she had.

She and the cat had bread and butter and milk pudding for lunch, and the cat perked up enough to make feeble attempts to wash while Loveday counted her money and did sums. The pair of them got into the chair presently and dozed until it was time to boil the kettle and make tea while the cat had the last of the rice pudding.

It was bordering on twilight when there was a

thump on the door. The cat got under the divan and after a moment there was another urgent thump on the door. Loveday went to open it.

'Hello,' said Dr Fforde. 'May I come in?'

He didn't wait for her to close her astonished mouth but came in and shut the door. He said pleasantly, 'That's a nasty eye.'

There was no point in pretending she didn't know who he was. Full of pleasure at the sight of him, and imbued with the feeling that it was perfectly natural for him to come and see her, she smiled widely.

'How did you know where I was?'

'I saw you at the hospital. I've come to ask a favour of you.'

'Me? A favour?' She glanced round her. 'But I'm hardly in a position to grant a favour.'

'May we sit down?' And when she was in the armchair he sat carefully on the old kitchen chair opposite. 'But first, may I ask why you are here? You were with Miss Cattell, were you not?'

'Well, yes, but I dropped a vase, a very expensive one...'

'So she slapped you and sent you packing?'

'Yes.'

'So why are you here?'

'Mrs Branch, she is Miss Cattell's cook, sent me here because Mrs Slade who owns it is her sister and I had nowhere to go.'

The doctor took off his specs, polished them, and put them back on. He observed pleasantly, 'There's a cat under the bed.'

'Yes, I know. He's starving. I'm going to look after him.'

The doctor sighed silently. Not only was he about to take on a mousy girl with a black eye but a stray cat too. He must be mad!

'The favour I wish to ask of you: my receptionist at my consulting rooms has had to return home at a moment's notice; would you consider taking her place until she returns? It isn't a difficult job—opening the post, answering the phone, dealing with patients. The hours are sometimes odd, but it is largely a matter of common sense.'

Loveday sat and looked at him. Finally, since he was sitting there calmly waiting for her to speak, she said, 'I can type and do shorthand, but I don't understand computers. I don't think it would do because of my eye—and I can't leave the cat.'

'I don't want you to bother with computers, but typing would be a bonus, and you have a nice quiet voice and an unobtrusive manner—both things which patients expect and do appreciate. As for the cat, I see no reason why you shouldn't keep it.'

'Isn't it a long way from here to where you work? I do wonder why you have come here. I mean, there must be any number of suitable receptionists from all those agencies.'

'Since Miss Priss went two days ago I have endured the services of a charming young lady who calls my patients "dear" and burst into tears because she broke her nail on the typewriter. She is also distractingly pretty, which is hardly an asset for a job such as I'm offering you. I do not wish to be distracted, and my patients have other things on their minds besides pretty faces.'

Which meant, when all was said and done, that Loveday had the kind of face no one would look at twice. Background material, that's me, thought Loveday.

'And where will I live?'

'There is a very small flat on the top floor of the house where I have my rooms. There are two other medical men there, and of course the place is empty at night. You could live there—and the cat, if you wish.'

'You really mean that?'

All at once he looked forbidding. 'I endeavour to say what I mean, Miss West.'

She made haste to apologise. 'What I really mean is that you don't know anything about me and I don't know anything about you. We're strangers, aren't we? And yet here you are, offering me a job,' she added hastily, in case he had second thoughts. 'It sounds too good to be true.'

'Nevertheless, it is a genuine offer of work—and do not forget that only the urgency of my need for adequate help has prompted me to offer you the job. You are at liberty to leave if you should wish to do so, providing you give me adequate time to find a replacement. If Miss Priss should return she would, of course, resume her work; that is a risk for you.' He smiled suddenly. 'We are both taking a risk, but it is to our advantage that we should help each other.'

Such terms of practicability and common sense made the vague doubts at the back of Loveday's head melt away. She had had no future, and now all at once security—even if temporary—was being handed her on a plate.

'All right,' said Loveday. 'I'll come.'

'Thank you. Could you be ready if I fetch you at half past eight tomorrow morning? My first patient is at eleven-thirty, which will give you time to find your way around.'

He stood up and held out a hand. 'I think we shall deal well with each other, Miss West.'

She put her hand in his and felt the reassuring firmness of it.

'I'll be ready—and the cat. You haven't forgotten the cat?"

'No, I haven't forgotten.'

CHAPTER TWO

LOVEDAY went to see Mrs Slade then, and in answer to that lady's doubtful reception of her news assured her that Dr Fforde was no stranger.

'Well, yer a sensible girl, but if you need an 'elping 'and yer know where to come.'

Loveday thanked her. 'I'll write to you,' she said, 'and I'll write to Mrs Branch too. I think it's a job I can manage, and it will be nice to have somewhere to live where I can have the cat.'

She said goodbye and went back to the basement, and, since a celebration was called for, she gave the cat half the cat meat and boiled two eggs.

In the morning she was a bit worried that the cat might try and escape, but the little beast was still too weak and weary to do more than cling to her when the doctor arrived. His good morning was businesslike as he popped her into the car, put her case into the boot and got in and drove away.

He was still glad to see her, but he had a busy day ahead of him and a day was only so long…

Loveday, sensing that, made no effort to talk, but sat clutching the cat, savouring the delight of being driven in a Bentley motor car.

His rooms were in a house in a quiet street, one in a terrace of similar houses. He ushered her into the narrow hall with its lofty ceiling and up the handsome staircase at its end. There were several doors on the landing, and as they started up the next flight he nodded to the end one.

'I'm in the end room. We'll go to your place first.'

They went up another flight of stairs past more doors and finally up a small staircase with a door at the top.

The doctor took a key from a pocket and opened it. It gave directly into a small room, its window opening onto the flat roof of the room below. There were two doors but he didn't open them.

'The porter will bring up your case. And I asked him to stock up your cupboard. I suggest you feed the cat and leave the window shut and then come down to my room. Ten minutes?'

He had gone, leaving her to revolve slowly, trying to take it all in. But not for long. Ten minutes didn't give her much time. She opened one of the doors and found a small room with just space for a narrow bed, a table, a mirror and a chair. It had a small window and the curtains were pretty. Still with the cat tucked under her arm, she opened the other door. It was a minute kitchen, and between it and the bedroom was an even smaller shower room.

Loveday sucked in her breath like a happy child and went to the door to see who was there. It was the porter with her case.

'Todd's the name, miss. I'm here all day until seven o'clock, so do ask if you need anything. Dr Fforde said you've got a cat. I'll bring up a tray and suchlike before I go. There's enough in the cupboard to keep you going for a bit.'

She thanked him, settled the cat on the bed and offered it food, then tidied her hair, powdered her nose and went down to the first floor, the door key in her pocket. She should have been feeling nervous, but there hadn't been time.

She knocked and walked in. This was the waiting room, she supposed, all restful greys and blues, and with one or two charming flower paintings on the walls. There was a desk in one corner with a filing cabinet beside it.

'In here,' said Dr Fforde, and she went through a half-open door to the room beyond where he sat at his desk. He got up as she went in.

He noticed with satisfaction that she looked very composed, as neat as a new pin, and the black eye was better, allowing for a glint of vivid green under the lid.

'I'll take you round and show you where everything is, and we will have coffee while I explain your work. There should be time after that for you to go around on your own, just to check things. As I told you, there are few skills required—only a smiling face for all the patients and the ability to cope with simple routine.'

He showed her the treatment room leading from his consulting room. 'Nurse Paget comes about ten o'clock, unless I've a patient before then. She isn't here every day, so she will explain her hours to you when you meet her. Now, this is the waiting room, which is our domain.'

Her duties were simple. Even at such short notice she thought that she would manage well enough, and there would be no one there in the afternoon so she would have time to go over her duties again. There would be three patients after five o'clock, he told her.

'Now, your hours of work. You have an early-morning start—eight o'clock—an hour for lunch, between twelve and one, and tea when you have half an hour to spare during the afternoon. You'll be free to leave at five o'clock, but I must warn you that frequently I have an evening patient and you would need to be here. You have half-day on Saturday and all Sunday free, but Miss Priss came in on Saturday mornings to get everything ready for Monday. Can you cope with that?'

'Yes,' said Loveday. 'You will tell me if I don't do everything as you like it?'

'Yes. Now, salary…' He mentioned a sum which made her blink the good eye.

'Too much,' said Loveday roundly. 'I'm living rent-free, remember.'

She encountered an icy blue stare. 'Allow me to make my own decisions, Miss West.'

She nodded meekly and said, 'Yes, Doctor,' but there was nothing meek about the sparkle in her eye. She would have liked to ask him to stop calling her Miss West with every breath, but since she was in his employ she supposed that she would have to answer to anything she felt he wished to call her.

That night, lying in her bed with the cat wrapped in one of her woolies curled up at her feet, Loveday, half asleep, went over the day. The two morning patients had been no problem; she had greeted them by name and ushered them in and out again, dealt with their appointments and filed away their notes and when the doctor, with a brief nod, had gone away, she had locked the door and come upstairs to her new home.

Todd had left everything necessary for the cat's comfort outside the door. She had opened the window onto the flat roof, arranged everything to her satisfaction and watched the cat creep cautiously through the half-open window and then back again. She'd fed him then, and made herself a cheese sandwich and a cup of coffee from the stock of food neatly stacked away in the kitchen.

The afternoon she had spent prowling round the consulting rooms, checking and re-checking; for such a magnificent wage she intended to be perfect...

The doctor had returned shortly before the first of his late patients, refused the tea she had offered to make him, and when the last one had gone he'd gone too, observing quietly that she appeared to have settled in nicely and bidding her goodnight. She had felt hurt that he hadn't said more than that, but had consoled herself with the thought that he led a busy life and although he had given her a job and a roof over her head that was no reason why he should concern himself further.

She had spent a blissful evening doing sums and making a list of all the things she would like to buy. It was a lengthy list...

Dr Fforde had taken himself off home. There was no doubt about it, Loveday had taken to her new job like a duck to water. His patients, accustomed to Miss Priss's austere politeness, had been made aware of the reason for her absence, and had expressed polite concern and commented on the suitability of her substitute. She might not have Miss Priss's presence but she had a pleasant manner and a quiet voice which didn't encroach…

He'd had an urgent call from the hospital within ten minutes of his return to his home. His work had taken over then, and for the time being, at least, he had forgotten her.

Loveday slept soundly with the cat curled up on her feet, and woke with the pleasant feeling that she was going to enjoy her day. She left the cat to potter onto the roof, which it did, while she showered and dressed and got breakfast. She wondered who had had the thoughtfulness to get several tins of cat food as she watched the little beast scoff its meal.

'You're beginning to look like a cat,' she told him, 'and worthy of a name.' When he paused to look at her, she added, 'I shall call you Sam, and I must say that it is nice to have someone to talk to.'

She made him comfortable on the woolly, left the window open and went down to the consulting room.

It was still early, and there was no one about except the porter, who wished her a cheerful good morning. 'Put your rubbish out on a Friday,' he warned her. 'And will you be wanting milk?'

'Yes, please. Does the milkman call?'

'He does. I'll get him to leave an extra pint and I'll put it outside your door.'

She thanked him and unlocked the waiting room door. For such a magnificent sum the doctor deserved the very best attention; she dusted and polished, saw to the flowers in their vases, arranged the post just so on his desk, got out the patients' notes for the day and put everything ready to make coffee. That done, she went and sat by the open window and watched the quiet street below. When the Bentley whispered to a halt below she went and sat down behind her desk in the corner of the room.

The doctor, coming in presently, glanced at her as he wished her a brisk good morning and sighed with silent relief. She hadn't been putting on a show yesterday; she really was composed and capable, sitting there sedately, ready to melt into the background until she was wanted.

He paused at his door. 'Any problems? You are quite comfortable upstairs?'

'Yes, thank you, and there are no problems. Would you like coffee? It'll only take a minute.'

'Please. Would you bring it in?'

Since she made no effort to attract attention to herself he forgot her, absorbed in his patients, but remembered as he left to visit those who were housebound or too ill to come and see him, to wish her good morning and advise her that he would be back during the afternoon.

Loveday, eating her lunchtime sandwich, leaning out of the window watching Sam stretched out in the autumn sunshine, told the cat about the morning's work, the patients who had come, and the few bad moments she had had when she had mislaid some notes.

'I found them, luckily,' she explained to him. 'I can't afford to slip up, can I, Sam? I don't wish Miss Priss to be too worried about her mother, but I do hope she won't come back until I've saved some money and found a job where you'll be welcome.'

Sam paused in his wash and brush-up and gave her a look. He was going to be a handsome cat, but he wasn't young any more, so a settled life would suit him down to the ground. He conveyed his feelings with a look, and Loveday said, 'Yes, I know, Sam. But I'll not part with you, I promise.'

At the end of the week she found an envelope with her wages on her desk, and when she thanked the doctor he said, 'I'll be away for the weekend. You'll be here in the morning? Take any phone calls, and for anything urgent you can reach me at the number on my desk. Set the answering-machine when you leave. I have a patient at half past nine on Monday morning.' At the door he paused. 'I hope you have a pleasant weekend.'

At noon on Saturday she locked the consulting rooms and went to her little flat. With Sam on her lap she made a shopping list, ate her lunch and, bidding him to be a good boy, set off to the nearest shops. The porter had told her that five minutes' walk away there were shops which should supply her needs. 'Nothing posh,' he said. 'Been there for years, they have, very handy, too.'

She soon found them, tucked away behind the rather grand houses: the butcher, the baker, the greengrocer, all inhabiting small and rather shabby shops, but selling everything she had on her list. There was a newsagent too, selling soft drinks, chocolates and sweets, and with a shelf of second-hand books going cheap.

Loveday went back to her flat and unpacked her carrier bags. She still wasn't sure when she could get out during the day, and had prudently stocked up with enough food to last for several days. That done, she sat down to her tea and made another list—clothes, this time. They were a pipe dream at the moment, but there was no harm in considering what she would buy once she had saved up enough money to spend some of it.

It was very quiet in the house. Todd had locked up and gone home, and the place would be empty now until he came again around six o'clock on Monday morning. Loveday wasn't nervous; indeed she welcomed the silence after Miss Cattell's voice raised unendingly in demands and complaints. She washed her hair and went to bed early, with Sam for company.

She went walking on Sunday, to St James's Park and then Hyde Park, stopping for coffee on the way. It was a chilly day but she was happy. To be free, with money in her purse and a home to go back to—what more could she ask of life? she reflected. Well, quite a bit, she conceded—a husband, children and a home...and to be loved.

'A waste of time,' said Loveday, with no one to hear her. 'Who would want to marry me in the first place and how would I ever meet him?'

She walked on briskly. He would have to love her even though she wasn't pretty, and preferably have enough money to have a nice home and like children. Never mind what he looked like... She paused. Yes, she did mind—he would need to be tall and reassuringly large, and she wouldn't object to him wearing specs on his handsome nose...

'You're being ridiculous,' said Loveday. 'Just because he's the only man who has spoken to you for years.'

She took herself off back home and had a leisurely lunch—a lamb chop, sprouts and a jacket potato, with a tub of yoghurt for pudding—and then sat in the little armchair with Sam on her lap and read the Sunday paper from front to back. And then tea, and later supper and bed.

'Some would call it a dull day, but we've enjoyed every minute of it,' she told Sam.

The week began well. The nurse, whom she seldom saw, had treated her with coolness at first, and then, realising that Loveday presented no risk to her status, became casually friendly. As for Dr Fforde, he treated her with the brisk, friendly manner which she found daunting. But such treatment was only to be expected....

It was almost the end of the week when he came earlier than usual to the consulting rooms. She gave him coffee and, since she was for the moment idle, paused to tell him that Sam had turned into a handsome cat. 'And he's very intelligent,' she added chattily. 'You really should come up and see him some time...'

The moment she had uttered them she wished the words unsaid. The doctor's cool, 'I'm glad to hear that he has made such a good recovery,' uttered in a dismissive voice sent the colour into her cheeks. Of course the very idea of his climbing the stairs to her little flat to look at the cat was ridiculous. As though he had the slightest interest...

She buried her hot face in the filing cabinet. Never, *never*, she vowed, would she make that mistake again.

Dr Fforde, watching her, wondered how best to explain to her that visiting her at the flat would cause gossip—friendly, no doubt, but to be avoided. He decided to say nothing, but asked her in his usual grave way to telephone the hospital and say that he might be half an hour late.

'Mrs Seward has an appointment after the last patient. She is not a patient, so please show her in at once.'

The last patient had barely been shown out when Mrs Seward arrived. She was tall, slender, with a lovely face, skilfully made up, and wearing the kind of clothes Loveday dreamed of. She had a lovely smile, too.

'Hello—you're new, aren't you? What's happened to Miss Priss? Has Andrew finished? I'm a bit early.'

'Mrs Seward? Dr Fforde's expecting you.'

Loveday opened his door and stood aside for Mrs Seward to go in. Before she closed it she heard him say, 'Margaret—this is delightful.'

'Andrew, it's been so long...' was Mrs Seward's happy reply.

Loveday went back to her desk and got out the afternoon patients' notes. That done, she entered their names and phone numbers into the daily diary. It was time for her to go to her lunch, but she supposed that she should stay; they would go presently and she could lock up. He would be at the hospital during the afternoon, and there were no more patients until almost four o'clock.

She didn't have long to wait. They came out together presently, and the doctor stopped at the desk and asked her to lock up. 'And since the first patient is at four o'clock there's no need for you to come back until three.'

His voice was as kind as his smile. Mrs Seward smiled too. On their way down to the car she said, 'I like your receptionist. A mouse with green eyes.'

The extra hour or so for lunch wasn't to be ignored. Loveday gobbled a sandwich, fed Sam, and went shopping, returning with her own simple needs and weighed down by tins of cat food and more books. She had seen that the funny little shop squeezed in between the grocer and the butcher sold just about everything and had noticed some small, cheap radios. On pay day, she promised herself, she would buy one. And the greengrocer had had a bucketful of chrysanthemums outside his shop; they perhaps weren't quite as fresh as they might have been, but they would add a cheerful splash of colour in the flat.

The doctor arrived back five minutes before his

patient, accepted the cup of tea she offered him and, when the last patient of the afternoon had gone, bade her goodnight without loss of time.

'They'll go out this evening,' said Loveday aloud. 'To one of those restaurants with little lamps on the tables. And then they'll go dancing. She's quite beautiful. They make a handsome pair.'

She locked up with her usual care and went upstairs to give Sam his supper and herself a pot of tea. She would have a pleasant evening, she told herself: an omelette for her supper and then a peaceful hour with one of the second-hand books.

'I'm becoming an old maid,' said Loveday.

There was news of Miss Priss in the morning; her mother was recovering from her stroke but must stay in hospital for another ten days. After that she would return home and be nursed by Miss Priss and a helper. There was every chance that she would recover, and then Miss Priss would be able to return to work once arrangements for her mother's comfort could be made.

The doctor told Loveday this without going into details, and although she was sorry for Miss Priss and her mother, she couldn't help feeling relief. She had known that sooner or later Miss Priss would be back, but the longer she could stay the more money she could save, and with some experience and a reference from the doctor she would have a better chance of finding work. She must remember, she told herself, to curb her tongue and not talk about herself or Sam.

As a result of this resolution the doctor was at first faintly amused and then puzzled at her wooden politeness towards him. She had become in the short time she had been working for him almost as efficient as Miss Priss; she was discreet, pleasantly attentive to his patients, willing to come early and work late if need be, and disappeared to her little flat so quietly that he barely noticed her going. And always there when he arrived in the mornings. It was what he expected and what he paid her for, but all the same he now had a vague sense of disquiet, so that he found himself thinking about her very frequently.

A few days later she went down rather earlier; there were more patients than usual today. The doctor would expect everything to be ready for them.

There was a man on the landing outside the consulting rooms, standing easily, hands in pockets, looking out of the landing window. He turned round to look at her as she reached the door.

He smiled at her and said good morning. 'I hoped someone would come soon. I'd love a cup of coffee.' At her surprised look, he added, 'Oh, it's quite all right, Andrew won't mind.'

When she still stood there, looking at him, he added impatiently, 'Open up, dear girl.'

'Certainly not,' said Loveday. 'I don't know

who you are, and even if you told me I'm not to know whether it's the truth. I'm so sorry, but if you want to see the doctor then you should come back at nine o'clock.'

She put the key in the lock. 'I have no intention of letting you in.'

She whisked herself inside, locked the door again and left him there. He had been sure of himself, demanding coffee, behaving as if he knew the doctor, but he could so easily be intent on skulduggery…

She set about her morning chores and had everything just as the doctor liked and the coffee ready when he came in.

The young man was with him and they were both laughing.

The doctor's good morning was said in his usual quiet manner, but his companion told Loveday, 'You see, I am a bona fide caller. Are you not remorseful at your treatment of me? And I only asked to be let in and given coffee.'

'You could have been a thief,' said Loveday.

'Quite right, Loveday,' interposed the doctor. 'You did the right thing and, since my cousin hasn't the good grace to introduce himself, I must do it for him. Charles Fforde, this is Miss Loveday West, who is my most efficient receptionist.'

Charles offered a hand, and after a tiny pause she shook it.

'What happened to Miss Prissy?'

'I'll tell you about her. Come into my room. There is time for coffee, but you must go away before my patients arrive.' The doctor opened his door. 'I should be free about one o'clock; we'll have lunch together.'

Loveday fetched the coffee. Charles was much younger than the doctor—more her own age, she supposed. He was good-looking too, and well dressed. She thought uneasily that he was very like Miss Cattell's men-friends, only younger. On the other hand he was the doctor's cousin, and he, in her view, was beyond reproach.

Charles didn't stay long, and on his way out he paused by her desk.

'Did anyone ever tell you that you have very beautiful eyes? The rest of you is probably charming, though hardly breathtaking, but the eyes…!'

He bent down and kissed the end of her nose.

'Till we meet again,' he told her, and reached the door in time to hold it open for the first patient.

No one had ever told Loveday that her eyes were beautiful. She savoured that for the rest of the day and tried to forget his remark about not being breathtaking. It had been so long since anyone had passed a remark about her appearance that she found it hard to ignore.

That evening, getting ready for bed, she examined her face carefully. 'Hardly breathtaking' was a kind way of saying plain…

All the same she took extra pains with her face and hair in the morning, and made plans to buy a new dress on Saturday afternoon.

If she had hoped to see Charles the next day

she was disappointed. There was no sign of him, and Dr Fforde, beyond his usual pleasant greeting, had nothing to say. All the same, she spent Saturday afternoon searching for a dress. It had to be something that would last. She found it after much searching: a navy blue wool crêpe, well cut and elegant, with the kind of neckline which could be dressed up by a pretty scarf. She bore it back and tried it on with Sam for a rather bored audience.

And on Monday morning she wore it to work.

Dr Fforde, wishing her his usual pleasant good morning noticed it immediately. It was undoubtedly suitable for her job, but it hardly enhanced her appearance. Her pretty mousy hair and those green eyes should be complemented by rich greens and russet, not buried in navy blue. He thought it unlikely that she had many friends, and perhaps none close enough to point this out to her. A pity. He sat down at his desk and started to go through his post.

* * *

It was Charles who voiced this same opinion when he came again during the week. He sauntered in after the last of the morning patients had gone and stopped at her desk.

'A new dress', he said as he eyed her up and down in a friendly fashion. 'In excellent taste too, dear girl, but why hide your charms behind such a middle-aged colour? You should be wearing pink and blue and emerald-green, and all the colours of the rainbow…'

'Not if she is to remain my receptionist,' said the doctor from his door, so that Loveday's wide smile at the sight of Charles was quenched. She contrived to look faintly amused, although her eyes sparkled green fire. The phone rang then and she turned to answer it, and the two men went into the consulting room together.

She had been delighted to see Charles, and although he didn't like the new dress he had said it was hiding her charms—which sounded old-fashioned but pleasant. And then Dr Fforde had to spoil it all. Who knew what Charles would have said if they had been left alone?

Loveday, a level-headed girl, realised that she was behaving in a way quite unlike her usual self-contained self. 'Which won't do,' she muttered as the phone rang again. And no one could have looked more efficient and at the same time inconspicuous than she did as Dr Fforde and Charles came into the room again.

'I shall be at the hospital until five o'clock,' the doctor told her. 'Have the afternoon off, but please be here by half past four.'

So Loveday had a leisurely lunch and decided to do some more shopping. She didn't need much, but she seldom had the chance to go out during the day and it was a bright day even if chilly. She got into her jacket—navy blue again, and bought to last—and with her shopping basket over one arm went out.

She had only gone a few yards down the street when she met Charles.

He took her arm. 'How about a walk in the park and tea? It's a splendid afternoon for exercise.'

She didn't try to conceal her pleasure at seeing him again. 'It sounds lovely, but I'm going shopping.'

'You can shop any day of the week.' He had tucked one arm into hers. 'Half an hour's brisk walk, then tea, and then if you must shop…'

'I have to be back by half past four.'

'Yes, yes. That's almost three hours away.'

He was laughing at her and, despite her good resolutions, she smiled back. 'A walk would be nice…'

He was an amusing companion and, bored with having nothing much to do for the moment, he found it intriguing to attract this rather sedate girl who had no idea how to make the most of herself. He had charm and a light-hearted way of talking, uncaring that he rarely meant a word of what he uttered. Those who knew him well joined in his cheerful banter and didn't take it seriously, but Loveday wasn't to know that…

He took her to a small café near the park, plied her with cream cakes and called her dear girl, and when they parted outside the consulting rooms he begged her to see him again. He touched the tip of her nose very gently as he spoke and his smile was such that she agreed at once.

'But I'm only free on Saturday afternoons and Sundays.'

'Sunday it shall be. We will drive into the country and walk and talk and eat at some village pub.' He turned away. 'Ten o'clock?'

'He didn't wait for her reply, which just for a moment she found disturbing, but she brushed that aside. A day out in his company would be lovely.

Dr Fforde, coming back just before five o'clock, wondered what had given Loveday a kind of inner glow; she was no longer insignificant, and her ordinary face was alight with happiness.

He asked, 'You enjoyed your afternoon?'

'Yes, thank you, Doctor.' Her beaming smile included him in her happiness, and for some reason that made him uneasy.

At breakfast on Sunday morning, Loveday explained to Sam that she would be away for the day. 'Well, most of it, I hope.' She added, 'But I won't be late home.' She kissed his elderly head. 'Be a good boy.'

Charles had said a drive into the country and a village pub. Her jacket and a skirt would be quite suitable; she would wear her good shoes and the pale blue sweater...

She was ready and waiting when she heard the silence of the quiet street disturbed by the prolonged blowing of his car's horn. She reached his car just as he was about to blow it again. 'Oh, hush,' she begged him. 'It's Sunday morning.'

He had looked faintly impatient, but now he laughed. 'So it is and we have the whole day before us.' He leaned across and opened the car door. 'Jump in.'

His car was a sports model, scarlet and flashy. She suppressed the instant thought that Dr Fforde's car was more to her liking and settled down beside Charles.

'It's a lovely morning,' she began.

'Marvellous, darling, but don't chatter until we are out of London.'

So she sat quietly, happy just to be there, sitting beside him, leaving the streets and rows of houses behind for a few hours.

He drove south, through Sevenoaks, and she wondered where they were going. They were well clear of London by now, but he had nothing much to say until he asked suddenly, 'Have you any idea where we're going?'

'No, except that it's south—towards the coast.'

'Brighton, darling. Plenty to do and see there.'

She had expected a day in the country—he had mentioned a country pub. Surely Brighton wasn't much different from London? But what did it matter where they went? She was happy in his company and he made her laugh...

He parked at the seafront and they had coffee and then walked, first by the sea and then through the town, stopping to look at the shop windows in the Lanes. Charles promised her that the next time they came he would take her to the Pavilion. They had lunch in a fashionable pub and then walked again, and if it wasn't quite what she had expected it didn't really matter. She was having a lovely day out and Charles was a delightful companion, teasing her a little, letting her see that he liked her, and telling her that he had never met a girl quite like her before. Loveday, hopelessly ignorant of the fashionable world, believed every word of it.

They drove back to London after a splendid tea in one of the seafront hotels.

'Do you come here often?' Loveday wanted to know.

Charles gave her his charming smile. 'Never with such a delightful companion.' He might have added, And only because here I'm most unlikely to meet anyone I know. He wasn't doing any harm, he told himself. Loveday led a dull life; what could be kinder than to give her a taste of romance? And it would keep him amused for the next few weeks...

She was a dear little thing, he reflected as they drove back, but too quiet and dull for him. It amused him to see how she blossomed under his attention.

'We must do this again,' he told her. 'I'll be away next weekend, but there's a good film we might go to see one evening. Wednesday. I'll come for you about half past seven.'

'I'd like that, thank you,' she said. And, Loveday being Loveday, she added, 'I won't need to dress up? I haven't anything smart to wear.'

'No, no. You look very nice.'

He turned his head to smile at her. She was

wearing something dull and unflattering, but the cinema he had in mind was well away from his usual haunts and he wasn't likely to see anyone who knew him.

He didn't get out of the car when they got back, but kissed her cheek and told her what a marvellous day it had been and then drove away before she had the key in the door. He had cut things rather fine; he had barely an hour in which to change for the evening.

Loveday climbed the stairs to the flat, to be met by an impatient Sam. She fed him and made a pot of tea before sitting down to drink it while she told him about her day. 'He's so nice,' she told Sam. 'He makes me laugh, and he makes me feel pretty and amusing although I know I'm not. We're going out again on Wednesday evening and I wish I had some pretty clothes to wear. He said it doesn't matter but I'd like to look my best for him. He notices what I'm wearing.' She sighed. 'Dr Fforde doesn't even see me—not as a girl, that is, only as his receptionist. And why I should think of him, I don't know.'

She was wrong, of course. Dr Fforde, coming to his rooms on Monday morning, at once saw the inner glow in Loveday's face and the sparkle in her eyes.

CHAPTER THREE

THE doctor bade her good morning and paused long enough to ask her if she had had a good weekend. 'You have friends to visit?' he wanted to know.

'Me? No. I hadn't time to make friends when I was with Miss Cattell,' she told him cheerfully.

So who or what had given her ordinary face that happy look? He went into his consulting room, thinking about it. It would hardly do for him to ask her how she spent her spare time, although he had a strong inclination to know that. Besides, it would be difficult to ask because her manner towards him had a distinct tinge of reserve. Probably she thought him too elderly to have an interest in her private life. A man approaching forty must seem middle-aged to a girl in her twenties.

He sat down to open his post and glanced up briefly when she came in with his coffee. The happy look was still there…

It seemed to Loveday that Wednesday took a long time in coming, and when it did she was in a fever of impatience; the last patient of the afternoon was elderly, nervous and inclined to want her own way, demanding a good deal of attention from the nurse and then sitting down again to repeat her symptoms once again to a patient Dr Fforde.

It was long after five when Loveday ushered her out, and it was almost an hour later when the nurse and Dr Fforde had gone too and she was at last ready to leave herself.

She sped up to the flat, fed an impatient Sam, made tea for herself and gobbled a sandwich left over from her lunch. She was hungry, but that was a small price to pay for an evening with Charles. She showered, changed into the jacket, skirt and a cream silk blouse, did her face with unusual care, brushed her mousy hair smooth and decided against her only hat. At least her shoes and handbag were good, even if they were no longer new.

She glanced out of the window; he would be here at any moment and he had been impatient on Sunday. She gave Sam a hug, locked up and hurried down to the street. She was just in time as Charles drew up.

He leaned over and opened the car door. 'There you are, darling. How clever of you to know that I hate being kept waiting.' When she had settled into the seat beside him he dropped a careless kiss on her cheek. She really was quite a taking little thing; it was a pity she dressed in such a dull fashion.

The film was just released, a triumph of modern cinema and Loveday, who hadn't been to the cinema for a long time, enjoyed it. When it ended and they had reached his car her heart lifted when he said, 'A drink and something to eat? It's still early.'

Eleven o'clock at night was late for her, now that she no longer had to keep the erratic hours Miss Cattell's household were obliged to put up with, and she had been going to her bed well before eleven. But she cast good sense to the winds and agreed.

To be disappointed. She was hungry, but Charles, it seemed, had dined earlier that evening, so 'drinks' were indifferent coffee and a bowl of nuts and tiny cheese biscuits in the bar of a nearby hotel. Not the usual hotel Charles frequented, and he made no attempt to dally over them. Loveday could see that he was anxious to be gone, and since she was by now as attracted to him as he had intended, she declared that she should go back to the flat.

'It's been a lovely evening,' she told him, 'and thank you for taking me.'

'My dearest girl, the pleasure was all mine.' He stopped before the consulting rooms, leaned across to open her door and then put an arm around her to kiss her. A sweet little thing, he reflected, but he was becoming the littlest bit bored with her. All the same he said, 'We must have another day out soon.'

He drove off, leaving her on the pavement. Loveday, unlocking the door, told herself that he must have had an urgent reason to rush away like that, and drowned the thought in the prospect of another day out with him.

'I have never been so happy,' she told Sam, eating her late supper of scrambled eggs on toast. And she was sure that she was. A nameless, niggling doubt at the back of her mind was easily lost in the remembrance of his kiss.

She made a mistake in the case notes in the morning, and forgot to give Dr Fforde a message from the hospital. Not an urgent one, but all the same there had been no excuse for forgetting it—except that she had been thinking of Charles.

The doctor accepted her apology with a nod and said nothing, but back in his home that evening he sat for a long time thinking about it.

Loveday was very careful during the next few days not to make any more mistakes. Never mind her vague dreams of a blissful future; the present was reality—security, a roof over her head, money in her pocket. Her scrupulous attention to her duties and her anxiety to please the doctor he found at first amusing, then puzzling. He didn't pretend to himself that he wasn't interested in her, but he was a man of no conceit and found it unlikley that a girl of her age, even if she was as level-headed as Loveday was, would wish to make a friend of a man so much older than she. He could only hope that whoever it was who had brought that look into her face would make her happy.

Charles phoned one morning during the week. Loveday had the place ready, the coffee set for the doctor and everything prepared for the day's work.

'Darling,' said Charles over the phone, 'I

thought we might have a lovely evening on Saturday. Wear a pretty dress; we'll dine and dance.'

He hung up before she could reply.

It seemed that Saturday would never come. When it did she got up early and went down to the consulting rooms; she set everything to rights ready for Monday before hurrying to get a bus which would take her to Oxford Street.

She had raided her nest egg, shutting her eyes to the fact that she was making a great hole in her secure future, but no one—no man—had ever asked her out to dine and dance before, and certainly not a man such as Charles, so full of fun and so obviously liking her a lot, perhaps even loving her...

It took her an hour or two to find what she wanted; a plain sheath of a dress, and well cut, although the material from which it was made was cheap—but the colour was right: a pale bronze which gave her hair colour and flattered her eyes. There was also money enough for shoes, found after much searching on a bargain rail in a cheap shoe shop. They weren't leather, though they looked as though they were, and they went well with the dress.

She hurried back home with her purchases to give Sam his tea before she boiled an egg and made a pot of tea for herself. Then she began to get ready for the evening. It was a pity that Charles hadn't said at what time he would call for her…

She was ready far too soon, and sat peering out of the window into the street below. Perhaps he had forgotten…

It was almost eight o'clock when she saw his car stop before the house, and Loveday, being Loveday, with no thought of keeping him waiting or playing hard to get, flew down to the door.

He was sitting in the car, waiting for her, and because she was living for the moment in a delightful dream world of her own his casual manners were unnoticed. She got into the car beside him and he put an arm round her and kissed her lightly.

'Got that pretty dress?' he wanted to know, and looked doubtfully at her coat; it was plain and serviceable and obviously not in the height of fashion.

'Yes.' She smiled at him. 'I bought it this morning.'

He had planned the evening carefully: dinner at a small restaurant in Chelsea—smart enough to impress her but hardly likely to entertain anyone he might know—and afterwards there was a dance hall not too far away. It was hardly a place he would consider taking any of his acquaintances, but he suspected that to Loveday it would be the highlight of their evening.

Their table was in the corner of the restaurant, a pleasant enough place, with shaded lights and its dozen or so tables already filled. The food was good too, and he ordered champagne. She could have sat there for ever opposite him, listening to his amusing talk, smiling happily at his admiring glances, but they didn't linger over dinner.

'I'm longing to dance with you,' Charles told her.

The dance floor was crowded and very noisy, and hemmed in by other dancers, they scarcely moved. For that Loveday was secretly thankful, as her opportunities to go dancing had been non-existent at Miss Cattell's home. She was disappointed but not surprised when he declared impatiently that dancing was quite out of the question.

'A pity,' he told her as they left the place. 'Having to cut short a delightful evening.'

There would be other evenings, thought Loveday, and waited for him to say so, only he didn't. Indeed, he didn't mention seeing her again as he drove her back. He was unusually silent, and once or twice she thought that he was on the point of telling her something.

'Is there anything the matter?' she asked.

'Matter? What on earth put that idea into your head?' He sounded angry, but then a moment later said, 'Sorry, darling, I didn't mean to snap. I wanted this evening to be something special.'

He stopped outside the consulting rooms and

turned to look at her. 'You wouldn't like to ask me up?'

'No, I wouldn't.' She smiled at him, and he put an arm round her shoulders and kissed her, then leaned forward to open her door.

She got out and turned to look at him. 'It was a lovely evening, Charles, thank you.' She waited for him to say something as she closed the door. But all he did was lift a hand in farewell and drive off. She stood on the pavement for a moment, disappointed that he hadn't said when they would meet again, and vaguely disturbed about it, but the memory of his kiss blotted uneasiness away. She unlocked the door and let herself into the house.

Dr Fforde, wanting some notes he had left in his consulting room, had walked round from his house, found them, put out his desk light, and was on his way through the waiting room when the sound of a car outside sent him to the window. He stood there, watching Loveday get out of the car, Charles drive away and her stillness before she turned to go into the house. He went then to open the door and switch on the landing light.

'Loveday.' His voice was reassuringly normal. 'I came to collect some notes I needed. 'I'm on my way out.'

He came down the stairs, switching on lights as he came, and found her standing in the hall.

'I've been out,' said Loveday unnecessarily, and added for good measure, 'With Charles.'

'Yes, I saw you and the car from the window. You've had a pleasant evening?'

She smiled at him. She would have liked to have told him all about her and Charles. He was, she reflected, the kind of person you wanted to tell things to. Instead she said happily, 'Oh, I had a lovely time,' and then, because she wanted to make it all quite clear, 'Charles has taken me out several times—we—seem to get on well together.'

Dr Fforde put his hand on the door. He smiled, but all he said was, 'Sleep well!'

In the flat, she told Sam all about it. 'I'm not

sure if Dr Fforde likes me going out with Charles. He's too nice to say so...'

She hung the pretty dress away and wondered when she would wear it again. Soon, she hoped.

She was used to being lonely. Sunday passed happily enough, with attending church and a walk, then back to Sam's company and the Sunday papers. Monday couldn't come quickly enough—there was sure to be a phone call from Charles. She counted her money once again. Perhaps a long skirt and a pretty top would be an asset? Something she could wear which wasn't too noticeable? They would probably go dancing again, somewhere quieter—the dance hall hadn't been the kind of place Charles would normally visit, she thought, but of course it had been near the restaurant.

Her spirits dwindled with the passing days. She went about her work quietly, careful not to make mistakes, passed the time of day with Nurse, answered the doctor when he spoke to her in her usual quiet way, but by the end of the week the happiness he had seen in her face was subdued.

It was on Thursday evening after the last patient had gone that he called her into his consulting rooms.

He was standing by the window looking down into the street below. He said over his shoulder. 'Loveday, there is something you should know...'

Miss Priss was coming back! She swallowed a sudden rush of feelings and said politely, 'Yes, Doctor?'

He turned to look at her. He said in a harsh voice, 'Charles is to be married in two weeks... his fiancée has been in America. You are unaware of this?'

She nodded, and then said, 'If you don't mind, I'd like to go to the flat. I'll clear up later.' Her voice didn't sound quite like hers, but it was almost steady. On no account must she burst into tears or scream that she didn't believe him. Dr

Fforde wasn't a man to tell lies—lies to turn her world upside down.

He didn't speak, but opened the door for her. And when she looked up at him and whispered, 'Thank you,' from a pale face, the kindness of his smile almost overset her.

She let herself into the flat and, almost unaware of what she was doing, fed Sam, made tea and sat down to drink it. This was a nightmare from which she would presently wake, she told herself. She was still sitting there, the tea cold in front of her, Sam looking anxious on her lap, when the flat door opened and Dr Fforde came in.

'I have a key,' he observed. 'I think you will feel better if you talk about it.' He glanced at the tea. 'We will have tea together and while we drink it we can discuss the matter.'

He put the kettle on and made fresh tea, found clean cups and saucers and put a nicely laid tray on the table between them. Loveday, watching him wordlessly, felt surprise at the ease with which he performed the small household duty.

He poured the tea and put a cup in front of her. 'Tell me about it—Charles has been taking you out? You began to feel that he was falling in love with you?' He added, 'Drink your tea.'

She sipped obediently. There was no reason why she should answer him, for this was her own business, none of his, and yet she heard herself say meekly, 'Not very often. Once or twice to the cinema and a day in the country and last Saturday evening.' She said in a voice thick with tears, 'I've been a silly fool, haven't I?'

'No,' he said gently. 'How were you to know if Charles didn't tell you? I don't suppose he deliberately set out to hurt you. He has fallen in and out of love many times, but he is to marry a strong-minded American girl who will make sure that he loves only her. He was having a last fling. He has been selfish and uncaring and has probably already forgotten you. That sounds harsh, but the obvious thing is to forget him, too. Believe me, you will, even though at the moment you don't believe me.'

Loveday wiped her hands across her wet eyes like a child. 'How could I have been so stupid? You have only to look at me. I'm not even a little bit pretty and I wear all the wrong clothes.' She suddenly began to cry again. 'I bought that dress just for the evening because he said I ought to wear pretty colours!' She gulped and sniffed. 'Please will you go away now?'

'No. Go and wash your face and do your hair and get a coat. We will have our supper together.' He glanced at his watch. 'Mrs Duckett, my housekeeper, will have it ready in half an hour or so. You will eat everything put before you and then I shall bring you back here and you will go straight to bed and sleep. In the morning your heart will be sore, and perhaps a little cracked, but not broken.'

He sounded so kind that she wanted to weep

again. 'I'm not hungry…' But all the same she went to the bedroom and did her hair, and the best she could with her poor pink-nosed face and puffy eyelids. Presently she went back to where he was waiting, the tea things tidied away and Sam on his knee.

She hadn't expected the house in the mews, a rather larger one than its neighbours, with windows on either side of its front door flanked by little bay trees. He ushered her into the narrow hall and Mrs Duckett came to meet them.

'This is my receptionist, Miss Loveday West,' said the doctor. 'She has had an upsetting experience and it seemed to me that one of your splendid suppers would make her feel better, Mrs Duckett. Loveday, this is my housekeeper, Mrs Duckett.'

Loveday shook hands and the housekeeper gave her a motherly look. Been crying her eyes out, by the look of it, she reflected, and took the coat the doctor had taken from Loveday.

'Ten minutes or so.' She beamed at them both. 'Just nice time for a drop of sherry.'

The doctor opened the door and pushed Loveday gently ahead of him. The room had a window at each end and there was a cheerful fire burning in the elegant fireplace between them. It was a charming room, with sofas on each side of the hearth, a Pembroke table between them and several bookshelves crowded with books. There was a long-case clock in one corner, and the whole room was lighted by shaded lamps on the various small tables.

'Come by the fire,' said the doctor. 'Do you like dogs?'

When she nodded she saw two beady eyes peering from a shock of hair, watching her from a basket by a winged armchair by the window.

'A dog—he's yours?'

'Yes. He stays in his basket because he's been hurt.' Dr Fforde bent to stroke the tousled head. 'He got knocked down in the street and no one owns him.'

'You'll keep him?'

'Why not? He's a splendid fellow and will be perfectly fit in a week or so.' He had poured sherry and offered her a glass. 'He has two broken legs. They're in plaster.'

'May I stroke him?'

'Of course. I don't think he's had much kindness in his life so far.'

Loveday knelt by the basket and offered a hand, and then gently ran it over the dog's rough coat. 'He's lovely. What do you call him?'

'Can you think of a suitable name? I have had him only a couple of days.'

She thought about it, aware that beneath this fragile conversation about the dog there was hidden a great well of unhappiness which at any minute threatened to overflow.

'Something that sounds friendly—you know, like a family dog with a lot of children.' She paused, thinking that sounded like nonsense. 'Bob or Bertie or Rob.'

'We will call him Bob. Come and finish your sherry and we'll have our supper.'

She wished Bob goodbye, and he stuck out a pink tongue and licked the back of her hand. 'Oh, I do hope he'll get well quickly,' said Loveday.

She had expected supper to be a light evening meal, but it wasn't supper at all. It was dinner at its best, eaten in a small dining room, sitting on Hepplewhite chairs at a table covered with a damask cloth and set with silver and glass. There was soup from a Coalport soup plate, chicken, cooked deliciously in a wine sauce, potato purée and tiny sprouts, and one of Mrs Duckett's sherry trifles to follow.

The doctor poured a crisp white wine and maintained a steady flow of undemanding talk, giving her no chance to think about anything other than polite answers. They had coffee at the table before he drove her back to the consulting rooms, went up to the flat with her, switched on the lights, wished Sam an affable goodnight and went back down the stairs after bidding her a quiet goodnight. She tried to stammer out her thanks but he waved them aside.

'I'll see you in the morning, Loveday,' he told her. 'Go to bed and go to sleep.'

And, strangely enough, that was what she did. She woke early, though, and her unhappiness, held at bay the evening before, took over. But now, in the light of the morning, she was able to think about it with a degree of good sense. She saw now that she had behaved like a lovesick teenager—just the kind of silly girl Charles had needed to keep him amused while his future wife was away.

That didn't make her unhappiness any the less. She had her dreams and she had been carried away by what she had supposed was Charles's delight in her company. She told herself that it was because she had been so little in a man's company that she had mistaken his attentions for real feeling. This was a sensible conclusion, which none the less didn't stop her crying her eyes out, so that she had to spend a long time doing things to her face before she went down to the consulting rooms.

She thought she had made rather a good job of it as she studied her face in the large mirror between the windows in the waiting room, but it was a good thing that she couldn't read the doctor's thoughts as he came in.

He noted the puffed eyelids and the still pink nose and the resolutely smiling mouth and reflected that she had one of the most unassuming faces he had ever seen. Except for those glorious eyes, of course. So what was it about her that took so much of his interest? An interest which he had felt the first time he had met her…

He went to his consulting room, accepted the coffee she brought him, and considered the matter. He was in love with her, of course; it was not a passing fancy. He had over the years considered marrying, and had, like any other man, fancied himself in love from time to time. But he had always known that the girl in question hadn't been the right one, that sooner or later he would meet a woman whom he would love and want to have for his wife. But now was hardly the time to tell Loveday that. Patience was called for, and he had plenty of that.

He had a busy day ahead of him, and would be spending the greater part of it at the hospital, so beyond giving Loveday instructions about patients and the time of his return, he had nothing to say. He could see that she was determined to keep her feelings concealed.

Only that evening, as he left to go home, he paused at her desk, where she was still busy.

'Bob spent half an hour in the garden this morning. You would be surprised at what he can manage to do on two legs and with a lot of help.'

She said gravely, 'He is a darling dog. I think he will be devoted to you; you saved his life.'

He smiled down at her. 'I think he will be a fine fellow once he is well again. Goodnight, Loveday.'

It was quiet after he had gone. It would be absurd, she told herself, to say that she missed him. She finished the tidying up and went upstairs to Sam's welcoming voice. She had got through the day, hadn't she? she reflected, and if she could get through one day she could get through as many more as she must before she could finally forget Charles.

The following week seemed endless; she listened to Nurse's confidences concerning her boyfriend with sympathy, presented a welcoming face to the doctor's patients, and carried on long one-sided conversations with Sam.

She planned her weekend with him. 'I shall go shopping on Saturday afternoon,' she told him, 'and on Sunday I'll go to church in the morning and then to Hyde Park in the afternoon, and we'll have a cosy evening together.'

And Sam, grown comfortably stout and placid,

got onto her lap and went to sleep. Life for him, at any rate, was quite perfect.

The last of Friday afternoon's patients came late. Nurse was annoyed because that meant she couldn't leave punctually, and just before the patient was ushered out the phone rang. Five minutes later Dr Fforde left too.

He bade the nurse goodnight, told Loveday to lock up and that he would be at the hospital, and went away.

Nurse followed him almost at once, grumbling because she would have to rush home and change before going out for the evening. 'And I wanted to get my hair done,' she complained, slamming the door behind her.

Which left Loveday alone, putting things to rights. She would be down in the morning to make sure that everything was ready for Monday, but all the same she liked to leave the place just so. She didn't hurry for she had no reason to do so, and even though after a week her unhappiness was dulled, her solitary evenings were the most difficult part of the day.

She spent longer than she needed in the consulting rooms the next morning, keeping her mind resolutely on prosaic things such as her shopping list and Monday's patients. The phone rang several times too—patients wanting to make appointments—and just as she was about to lock up, Mrs Seward rang.

'I know Fforde isn't there,' she told Loveday, 'but would you leave a message for him? Ask him to come and see me on Monday if he can manage it? If he knows before his morning patients he may be able to arrange something. Thank you. Am I talking to the girl with the green eyes?'

'Yes.'

'Miss Priss not back yet? I'm sure you're filling her shoes very competently. You won't forget the message?'

She rang off and Loveday thought what a

pleasant, friendly voice she had. Perhaps the doctor was going to marry her…

She was on the way upstairs to her flat when she heard the front door bang shut. It wouldn't be Todd, he used the entrance at the back of the house, and the three other medical men who had rooms there were all out of London for the weekend, Todd had told her that before he had gone home the previous evening.

Not quite frightened, but cautious, Loveday started down the stairs.

Dr Fforde was coming up them, two at a time. He stood on the landing, looking up at her.

'I'm glad I find you in,' he observed. 'Can you spare an hour later on today? Late afternoon, perhaps? I'll call for you around four o'clock. Bob is doing splendidly, but I fancy he needs some distraction—a new face. Will you come?'

'Well, if you think it might help him to get better quickly… He can't go out?'

'Into the garden. With two of us he might feel encouraged to hobble around in his plasters. He has forgotten how to enjoy life. Indeed, I think that he never had that opportunity.'

'Oh, the poor dog. Of course I'll come.'

'Good!' He was already going back downstairs. 'I'll see you later.'

'Oh, wait!' cried Loveday. 'I almost forgot. Mrs Seward phoned. She asked if you would arrange to see her on Monday; she wanted you to know as soon as possible when you got here on Monday morning.'

He nodded, said, 'Thanks,' and went on his way out of the house.

There would be no time to sit and brood; Loveday fed Sam, had a quick lunch, and hurried to the shops. They knew her there by now, with her modest purchases of lamb chops and sausages, tins of cat food, butter, tea and coffee, some greengrocery and a loaf and, last of all, another book or two. A nice, quiet little lady they told each other, and occasionally they popped something extra into her basket.

She went back in good time to do her hair and her face, and leave the ever-hungry Sam something to eat on his saucer, before going to the window to watch for the doctor's car. When it came, instead of waiting there for her to go down, he got out and came into the house and all the way to her flat to knock on her door.

She couldn't help but compare his easy good manners with Charles's careless ones, and a small shaft of pleasure shot through her as he ushered her into the car and closed the door.

Bob was pleased to see her, and instead of lying rather listlessly in his basket he made valiant efforts to sit up.

'Oh, you clever boy,' said Loveday. 'You're better! He is better?' she asked anxiously.

'Yes. The vet's pleased with him. It wasn't only the legs, he was in poor shape, but now he's getting his strength back. We'll go into the garden for a few minutes and you can see what he can do.'

The doctor carried the little dog outside and set him down gently, and after a few moments Bob dragged himself onto his two front legs. He wasn't sure what to do with the ungainly plastered back legs, but presently he stood, a bit wobbly, looking pleased with himself.

'Once he's discovered that he can use his legs without pain, even if they're clumsy, there'll be no holding him.' The doctor picked him up and carried him back indoors and settled Loveday in a chair by the fire.

'Shall we have tea? Bob loves company.'

Mrs Duckett's teas were like no other: there were muffins in a silver dish, tiny sandwiches, fairy cakes, and a cake thick with fruit and nuts. It was just the right meal for a chilly autumn day, sitting round the fire, talking of this and that, both of them perfectly at ease.

Dr Fforde, who was skilled in the art of extracting information from patients who were reluctant to give it, went to work on Loveday.

'No family?' he enquired casually. 'Surely someone—an aunt or uncle or cousin—even if you have little to do with them?'

He was an easy man to talk to. 'I was brought up by an aunt; she died some years ago. There's another aunt—my father's much older sister. She lives in a village on the edge of Dartmoor. We send each other cards at Christmas but I've never met her. I—I haven't liked to ask her if I might go and see her. I expect she thinks I have a satisfactory life here, and it's a long way. In any case, Miss Cattell didn't like me having a holiday. I hated being there, but it was a job, and I'm not trained for anything, am I?'

He agreed in a non-committal way. 'I have no doubt that you would have no difficulty in getting work. There is always a shortage of good receptionists. But you would like to visit your aunt?'

'Yes. Well, I mean, she is family, isn't she? If

you see what I mean? But I expect she's happy living in Devon and would hate to have her life disrupted, even for a brief visit.' She added, 'And I'm very happy here.'

He was looking at her so thoughtfully that she hurried to change the subject. 'This is a charming house. You must like coming home each day.'

'Indeed I do, but I'm fond of the country too. I don't know Dartmoor at all; it must be very different...'

The casualness of his remark encouraged her to say, 'Oh, I'm sure it is. My aunt lives in a small village, somewhere near Ashburton. Buckland-in-the-Moor. It sounds lovely, but I expect it's lonely. It's a long way away.'

The doctor, having obtained all the information he wanted, began to talk of Bob and his future, which led naturally enough to Sam, his intelligence, his appetite and his delightful company...

Loveday glanced at the clock. 'Heavens, it's almost six o'clock. If you don't mind, I'd like to go back to the flat. It's been lovely, but I've several things to do and the evenings go so quickly.'

Which wasn't true. They dragged from one hour to the next while she did her best to forget Charles's red car screaming to a halt below her window…

The doctor made no demur. She bade Bob goodbye, thanked the doctor for her tea and got back into the car. At the consulting rooms she began to say, 'You don't need to get out—'

She could have saved her breath; he went upstairs with her, opened the flat door and switched on the lights, and bade Sam a cheerful good evening before expressing, in the briefest manner, his thanks for her company.

'Bob was delighted to see you,' he assured her. He had been delighted too, but he wasn't going to say so.

Loveday, listening to his footsteps receding on the stairs, was aware of a loneliness worse than usual. 'It's because he's such a large man that I notice when he's not here,' she told Sam.

CHAPTER FOUR

IT WAS on Monday morning that she saw the doctor had given himself a day off on Wednesday. She guessed why at once. It would be Charles's wedding day—a guess confirmed presently when Nurse came. She had a glossy magazine under one arm.

'Look at this.' She found the page and handed it to Loveday. 'Remember Dr Fforde's young cousin, who came here a few weeks ago? He's getting married—here's his picture and that's his fiancée. Pretty, isn't she? They are going to live in America, lucky them. The wedding is on Wednesday—a big one—you know, huge hats and white satin and bridesmaids. I must say they make a handsome pair.'

She took the magazine back again. 'Dr Fforde will go—he's bound to, isn't he? They're cousins, even if he is a lot older.'

'She's very pretty,' said Loveday, and wished that the phone would ring so that she had an excuse not to stand there gossiping. And the phone did ring, so that Nurse went away to the dressing room which was her workplace. Since there was a busy day ahead of them there would be little chance of more chatting. Loveday heaved a sigh of relief and turned a welcoming smile onto the first patient.

But, busy or not, it was hard not to keep thinking of Charles. She knew now that the whole thing had been nothing but an amusing interlude to him, and if she hadn't led such a narrow life she would have recognised that and treated the whole affair in the same light-hearted manner. But knowing that didn't make it any easier to forget…

On Tuesday the doctor was at the hospital all day, returning at five o'clock to see two patients in his consulting rooms. It had been very quiet all day, although Loveday had been kept busy enough making appointments. It had been a good opportunity to sort through the papers scattered on the doctor's desk, tidy them into heaps and write one or two reminder notes for him. To-morrow he would be away all day, but since he had said nothing she supposed that she would be there as usual, taking calls and messages.

Neither patient stayed long, and it was barely six o'clock when she ushered the last one out and began to tidy up.

The doctor left soon after, but first he stopped to tell her that he had switched on the answer-ing-machine. 'Anything urgent will be referred to Dr Gregg,' he told her, 'and you need only be here between ten o'clock and noon, then again between five o'clock and six. I'll be in as usual on Thursday.' He smiled suddenly. 'Would you do something for me? Would you go to my house in the early afternoon and give Bob half an hour in the garden? Mrs Duckett is nervous of hurting him. He's managing very well now, but he does need someone there.' He added, 'That is, unless you have planned something?'

'No, no. I haven't. Of course I'll go and keep Bob company for a little while. Mrs Duckett won't mind?'

'Mrs Duckett will be delighted. Goodnight, Loveday.'

She would do her weekly shopping in the morning, Loveday decided, and go to the doctor's house around two o'clock. She sat down to make out her small list of groceries. 'And a tin of sardines for you,' she promised Sam.

The doctor's house was a brisk ten minutes' walk away. Loveday knocked on its elegant front door just after two o'clock and was admitted by a smiling Mrs Duckett.

'Bob's waiting for you. I told him you'd be here soon. He misses the doctor when he's not home. I'm fond of him, but I'm a bit nervous on account of his legs. Keep your coat on, miss, it'll be chilly in the garden. Half an hour, the doctor said, and then you're to have a cup of tea before you go.'

She bustled Loveday into the sitting room. 'Look at that, then. He's trying to get onto his legs he's that happy to see you.'

She opened the doors onto the garden and trotted away with the reminder that tea would be brought at three o'clock.

Loveday knelt and put an arm round Bob's shoulders. Now that he was fed and rested and belonged to someone he was quite handsome, although his looks could be attributed to a variety of ancestors. Not that that mattered in the least, she assured him.

She picked him up and took him into the garden, and once there he took heart and struggled around, dragging his cumbersome plastered legs, obviously glad of her company. After a time they went back to the house and sat companionably side by side, he in his basket, Loveday on the floor beside him. He was a splendid companion too, listening with every sign of interest while she told him about Charles getting married and how lucky he was to have such a kind master, and presently Mrs Duckett came with the tea tray. There was dainty china and a little silver teapot, crumpets in a covered dish, little cakes and wafer-thin bread and butter, and, of course, a biscuit for Bob.

Loveday enjoyed every morsel and strangely enough she didn't think about the wedding, only that tea would have been even nicer if the doctor had been there with them.

She left soon after and hurried back to the consulting rooms, then sat at her desk from five o'clock until the clock struck six, answering a few calls on the phone and making sure that everything was ready for the morning.

The doctor arrived punctually the next morning, and paused on his way to thank her for visiting Bob, but if she had hoped for him to mention the wedding she was to be disappointed. With the remark that they had a busy morning before them, he went into his consulting room and closed the door.

Watching Sam scoff his supper that evening, she wondered aloud if she would be asked on Friday morning to visit Bob at the weekend, but here again she was to be disappointed; beyond reminding her that he would be at the hospital on Monday morning and wishing her a pleasant weekend he had nothing to say.

'And why I should have expected anything else I have no idea,' said Loveday, expressing her thoughts, as usual, to Sam.

The weather had changed, becoming dull and wet and windy. All the same, she wrapped up warmly and went walking. Not to the shops; she might spend too much money if she did that, and the nest egg in the Post Office was growing steadily. It would have been even larger if she hadn't bought that dress…

She was beginning to feel secure; there had been no news of Miss Priss, and the weeks were mounting up. Her return had receded into a vague worry which was becoming vaguer every day.

She was in the consulting rooms in good time on Monday morning, for although the doctor might not be there there was plenty to do. She sorted the post and laid it ready on his desk, noting with a small sigh of relief that there was no envelope with Miss Priss's spiky writing on it.

That letter was in the doctor's pocket, for it had been sent to his house. He had read it and then read it again; Miss Priss's mother had died and she would be glad to return to work as soon as she had settled her affairs.

I shall give up our home. It is a rented house and I do not wish to remain here. Would you consider allowing me to live in the flat on the top floor of the consulting rooms?

I would be happy to receive a reduced salary in this case, or pay rent. I have no family and few friends here and must find somewhere to live. I would not have suggested this, but I have worked for you for so many years that I feel I can venture to give voice to this possible arrangement.

Of course he would agree to it; Miss Priss was a trusted right hand, had been for years, and the arrangement would give her a secure future and a home. She must be in her fifties, he thought, at a time in life when the years ahead should offer that security. A letter, reassuring her, must be written, and Loveday must be told.

The answer to Loveday, as far as he was concerned, was to marry her. But first he must allow her to get over Charles and, that done, he would wait until the cracks in her heart were healed. But in the meantime she would need a roof over her head…

He wrote reassuringly to Miss Priss: she was to have the flat and to resume her duties just as soon as she felt able. He suggested two weeks ahead. He would be delighted to have her back and she was to regard the flat as her home until such time as she might wish to leave.

The letter written, he turned his thoughts to Loveday. Before he told her, he decided, he would drive down to the remote village where her aunt lived.

The orderly days slid by and it seemed to him that Loveday was beginning to forget Charles. She was quiet, but then she always was; however, her face in repose was no longer sad.

Early on Saturday morning he started on the long drive to the village on Dartmoor with Bob propped up beside him. It would probably be a wild-goose chase but it was the obvious thing to do...

It was a journey of about two hundred miles, but once free of London and its sprawling suburbs the road was fairly empty, and the further west he went the emptier it became. On a quiet stretch of road he stopped for coffee and to see to Bob's needs, and then he drove on until he reached the bypass to Exeter and took the road to the moor. Presently he turned off and drove through Ashburton and into the empty country beyond. It was a clear late-autumn day and the majestic sweep of the moorland hills swept away from him into the distance. The road was narrow now, and sheep roamed to and fro between the craggy rocks. Bob, who had never seen a sheep, was entranced.

The village, when he reached it, was charming, built on the banks of the river Dart and surrounded by trees. It had a handful of grey stone houses and an ancient church, a cheerful-looking pub and one or two bigger houses near the church. The doctor stopped at the pub and went inside.

The bar was small and cosy, with a bright log fire burning and comfortable chairs set beside the tables. It would be a focal point in the village, he reflected, and a cheerful haven on a bleak winter's evening.

Of course he could have lunch, said the elderly man behind the bar. A pasty and a pint of the best ale in the country, and the dog was welcome to come in.

Bob, carried in and sat gently on the floor, caused quite a stir. The two young men playing darts abandoned their game to come and look at his plastered legs and an old man by the fire declared that he'd never seen anything like it before. Their interest in him engendered a friendly atmosphere and a still deeper interest when the doctor mentioned that he had driven down from London.

'Lost, are you?' one of the young men wanted to know.

'No, no. I've come to visit someone living here. A Miss West?'

'Up at Bates Cottage?' volunteered the landlord, setting down the pasty and a bowl of water for Bob. 'Know her, do you, sir? Elderly, like, and not given to visitors?'

He looked at the doctor with frank curiosity.

'I have never met her. I have come to see her on behalf of her niece.'

'Oh, aye, she's got a niece—sends her a card at Christmas. Me ma cleans for her and sees to her post and shopping. She told Miss West she should have her niece to stay, but the old lady's independent, like, don't want to be a nuisance.'

'I should like to go and see her this afternoon...'

'As good a time as any. It's the last house at the end of the lane past the church. Too big for her, but she won't move. Got her dogs and cats and birds.'

'Could you put me up for the night?' asked the doctor.

'That I can,' said the landlord. 'And you could do with a nice bit of supper, no doubt?'

'Indeed I could. I'll go and call on Miss West before it gets dark.' He paid his bill, ordered pints all round, picked up Bob and went back to the car. It was no distance to Miss West's house, but unless she invited Bob in he would have to stay in the car.

The house was built of grey stone and thatched, and it was a good deal larger than the other cottages in the village. The curtains were undrawn and in the beginnings of an early dusk the lamplight from the room beside the stout front door shone cheerfully.

He went up the path and tugged the old-fashioned bell.

The elderly lady who opened it was small and brisk.

'I'm Miss West. Are you looking for me? If so why? I don't know you.'

The doctor perceived that he would need his bedside manner.

'I apologise for calling upon you in this manner, but first I must ask you if you are indeed the aunt of Loveday West?'

She stood staring at him. 'Yes, I am. Come inside.' She peered past him. 'What is that in your car?'

'My dog.'

'Fetch him.'

'He has two legs in plaster and is somewhat of an invalid.'

'All the more reason to bring him inside.'

When he'd fetched Bob she led the way from the narrow hall to the sitting room, which was nicely lighted, warmed by a brisk open fire and comfortably furnished.

'While you are explaining why you have come to see me we may as well have tea. Sit there, near the fire—your dog can sit on the rug.'

The doctor did as he was told. 'His name is Bob.'

Now that he was in the lighted room he could see her clearly. She was in her late sixties or early seventies, he judged, and what she lacked in height she made up for by the strength of her personality. A lady to be reckoned with, he reflected, feeling a little amused, with her plain face, fierce dark eyes and iron-grey hair tugged back into an old-fashioned bun at the back of her head.

He sat down with Bob's head on his feet. He had liked the old lady on sight, but wondered if he was making a mistake. He would know that when he had told her about Loveday.

He got up and took the tea tray from her as she came back into the room. He set it on a small table, then waited until she had sat down before resuming his seat. Good manners came to him as naturally as breathing. Miss West, pouring the tea, liked him for that.

'If I might introduce myself?' suggested the doctor, accepting a cup of tea. 'Andrew Fforde—I'm a doctor. I have a practice in London and work at a London hospital.'

Miss West, sitting very upright in her chair, nodded. 'Give Bob a biscuit. Is he good with cats?'

'My housekeeper has a cat; they get on well together.'

'Then be good enough to open the kitchen door so that my cats and Tim can come in.'

He did as he was asked and three cats came into the sitting room. None of them in their first youth, they ignored Bob and sat down in a tidy row before the fire. Plodding along behind them was an odd dog, with a grey muzzle and a friendly eye, who breathed over Bob and sat down heavily on the doctor's feet.

Miss West passed him the cake dish. 'I have not seen Loveday since she was a very small girl. She wrote to me when her other aunt died. She made it plain that she was living in easy circumstances and has never asked for help of any kind. We exchange cards at Christmas. I have thought of her as one of these young women with a career and a wish to live their own lives without encumbrances of any sort.' She sipped her tea from a delicate china cup. 'Perhaps I have been mistaken?'

When he didn't answer, she said, 'Tell me what you have come to tell me.'

He put down his cup and saucer and told her. He added no embellishments and no opinions of his own, and when he had finished he added, 'It seemed to me right that you should know this...'

'Is she pretty?'

'No, I think perhaps one would call her rather plain. But she has a beauty which has nothing to do with looks. She has beautiful green eyes and soft mousy hair. She is small and she has a charming voice.'

'Fat? Thin?'

'Slim and nicely rounded.'

'You're in love with her?'

'Yes. I hope to marry her, but first she must recover from her meeting with Charles.'

Miss West stroked a cat which had climbed onto her lap. 'How old are you?'

'Thirty-eight. Loveday is twenty-four.'

'I like you, Dr Fforde. I don't like many people, and I have only just met you, nevertheless, I like you. Do whatever you think is the best for

Loveday, and bring her here until she is ready to go with you as your wife.'

'That will be for her to decide,' he said quietly. 'But if she chooses to go her own way, then I shall make sure that she has a good job and a secure future.'

Miss West said, 'You love her as much as that?'

'Yes.' He smiled at her. 'Thank you for seeing me and giving me your willing help. May I let you know if our plans will be possible? It depends upon Loveday.'

'If Loveday decides to come and stay with me I shall make her welcome. And I wish you luck, Dr Fforde.'

'Thank you.' He would need it, he reflected on his way back to the pub. He had no right to interfere in Loveday's life and she would probably tell him so…

The small bar was full, and although he was stared at with frank curiosity, they were friendly stares.

The landlord, drawing him a pint, asked cheerfully if he had found Miss West. 'Nice old lady—lived here for a lifetime, she has. Don't hold with travel. There's a steak pie and our own sprouts for your supper, sir. Seven o'clock suit you? And if you let me know what your dog will eat...?' He eyed Bob, braced against the doctor's legs. 'Nice little beast. Seeing as he's an invalid, like, I'll put an old rug in your room for him.'

The doctor slept soundly. He had done what he had come to do, though whether it was the right thing only time would tell.

As for Bob, he was with his master and that was all that mattered to him. He had had a splendid supper and the old rug was reassuringly rich in smells: of wood ash and spilt food and ingrained dirt from boots. Just the thing to soothe a dog to sleep.

The doctor left after an unhurried breakfast, taking his time over the return trip to London. He had a lot to think about and he could do that undisturbed. He stopped for coffee and to accommodate Bob's needs and then, since the road was almost empty, he didn't stop again until he reached home.

Mrs Duckett spent Sunday afternoons with her sister and the house was quiet. But there was soup keeping warm on the Aga and cold meat and salad set out on the kitchen table. There was a note from Mrs Duckett telling him that she would cook him his dinner when she returned later.

He fed Bob and went to his study, to immerse himself in work. There was always plenty of paperwork; even with the secretary who came twice a week his desk was never empty. It wasn't until a faint aroma of something delicious caused him to twitch his splendid nose that he paused. Mrs Duckett was back and he was hungry.

* * *

Loveday went to bed early in her little flat, happily unaware of the future which was to be so soon disturbed.

The next day the doctor was due to go to the hospital after he had seen his patients at the consulting rooms, and he would be there for the rest of the day, but there was almost half an hour before he needed to leave. He went into the waiting room and found Loveday filing away patients' notes and writing up his daily diary ready for the morning.

She looked up as he went in. 'I'll type those two letters and leave them on your desk,' she told him. 'If there's anything urgent I could phone you at the hospital?'

'Yes, I'm booked up for the morning, aren't I? Use your discretion and fit in patients where you can. Anything really urgent, refer them to me at the hospital. I shall be there until six o'clock at least.'

He leaned against the desk, looking at her. 'I had a letter from Miss Priss. Her mother has died and she asks to come back to work in ten days' time; she also asks if she might have the flat in which to live. She has no family and her mother's house was rented.'

Loveday had gone a little pale. 'I'm so sorry Miss Priss's mother has died. But I'm glad that she has somewhere to come to where she can make her home. When would you like me to leave?'

'In a week's time? That gives me ample opportunity to ask around and find another similar job for you. I know a great many people and it shouldn't be too difficult.'

She said quickly, 'That is very kind of you, but I'm sure that I can find work…'

He said harshly, 'You will allow me to help you? I have no intention of allowing you to be homeless and workless. You came here to fill an emergency at my request; you will at least allow me to pay my debt.'

'Isn't a week rather a short time? I mean to find another job for me? Besides, you're busy all day…'

It was just the opening he had hoped for. 'Perhaps it may take longer than a week. You told me that you have an aunt living in Devon. Would you go and stay with her until I can get you fixed up?'

'But I've never seen her, at least not since I was a very little girl, and she might not want to have me to stay. And it's miles away…'

He said quietly, 'I went to see your aunt on Saturday, after I received Miss Priss's letter. You see, Loveday, I had to think of something quickly. She is quite elderly and I liked her—and she is both eager and willing for you to stay with her until you can get settled again.'

'You went all that way to see my aunt? Your weekend wasted…?'

'Not wasted, and, as I said, I like to pay my debts, Loveday.'

He straightened up and went to the door. 'Will you think about it and let me know in the morning? It's a sensible solution to the problem, you know.'

He smiled at her then, and went away. He wanted very much to stay and comfort her, to tell her that she had no need to worry, that he would look after her and love her. Instead he had told her everything in a matter-of-fact voice which gave away none of his feelings. The temptation to cajole her into accepting his offer was great, but he resisted it. He wanted her to love him— but only of her own free will.

Loveday sat very still; she felt as though someone had hit her very hard on the head and taken away her power to think. She had managed to answer the doctor sensibly, matching his own matter-of-fact manner, but now there was no need to do that. A week, she thought—seven days in which to find a job. She would have to start finding it at once, for of course there was no question of her accepting his offer of help.

She began to cry quietly. Not because she was once more with an undecided future but because that future would be without him. This calm, quiet man who had come to her rescue and who, she had no doubt, once he had made sure that she had another job, would dismiss her from his mind. She gave a great sniff, wiping the tears away with the back of her hand. After all, he had Mrs Seward, hadn't he?

Loveday, who had never felt jealous in her life before, was suddenly flooded with it.

Presently she stopped crying; it was a waste of time and was of no help at all. She put away the rest of the patients' notes, and then, since she would have the afternoon to get things ready for the next day, she selected the most likely newspapers and magazines to contain job advertisements and took herself off to the flat.

She explained it all to Sam, who yawned and went back to sleep, so she made a pot of tea, cut a sandwich and sat down to look through the job vacancy columns. There were plenty of vacancies—all of them for those with computer skills or, failing that, willing to undertake kitchen duties or work in launderettes. Since she had no knowledge of computers it would have to be something domestic. And why stay in London? Since she wouldn't see the doctor again, the further away she got from him the better.

'Out of sight, out of mind,' said Loveday, and because she was unhappy, and a little afraid of the future, she started to cry again.

But not for long. Presently she restored her face to its normal, or almost normal appearance and went back to the consulting room. She tidied up and got everything ready for the next day, made several appointments too, and brought the daily diary up to date, and when Mrs Seward phoned during the afternoon she answered her in a pleasant manner.

It was hard to dislike Mrs Seward; she was friendly and she had a nice voice. She sighed when Loveday told her that the doctor was at the hospital.

'I'll ring there and see if I can leave a message,' she told Loveday, 'but leave a note on his desk, will you? It's not urgent, but I do want to talk to him.'

Loveday went to bed early, since sitting alone in the flat while her thoughts tumbled around in her head was of no use, but her last waking thought was that nothing would persuade her to accept the doctor's suggestion.

When she sorted out the post in the morning there was a letter for her. From her aunt.

It was a long letter, written in a spidery hand, and, typically of Miss West, didn't beat about the bush. She had had a visit from Dr Fforde and agreed with him that the sensible thing to do was for Loveday to spend a few days with her while suitable work was found for her.

It is obvious that he is a man who has influence and moreover feels that he is in-

debted to you, as indeed he is. We know nothing of each other, but I shall be glad of your company. We are, after all, family. I live very quietly, but from what I hear from Dr Fforde you are not one of these modern career girls. I look forward to seeing you.

There was a PS: *Bring your cat with you.*

Dr Fforde, wishing her good morning later on that day, noted that she had been crying, but her ordinary face, rather pink in the nose and puffed around the eyes, was composed.

'I have had a letter from my aunt, explaining that you have been to see her and inviting me to stay until I've another job.'

And when he didn't answer, but stood quietly, watching her, she said, 'I expect it would be more convenient to you if I go and stay with her. So may I leave on Saturday? I expect Miss Priss would like to come as soon as it can be arranged.' She gave him a brave smile which tore at his heart. 'If I go early on Saturday morning she could have the weekend to move in. I'll leave everything ready for her.'

'That sounds admirable. I will drive you down to your aunt on Saturday morning.'

She said quickly, 'No, no. There's no need. I haven't much luggage and I'm sure there is a splendid train service.'

'None the less I will drive you and Sam, Loveday.'

She knew better than to argue when he spoke in that quiet voice.

'Well, thank you. And if you will write and let me know if you hear of a job?' She added hastily, 'Oh, I'm sure you will, because you said so, but I could always go to Exeter. There is sure to be something there…'

She looked very young standing there, and he was so much older. He was sure she probably thought of him as middle-aged. He said gently, 'If you would trust me, Loveday…'

'Oh, I do. You must know that.'

He smiled then, and went to his consulting room.

Loveday and he would be leaving, she told Sam, and she bought a cat basket which he viewed with suspicion. He was suspicious too when she started to spring-clean the flat. The little place must be left pristine, she told herself.

It kept her busy when she wasn't at work, so that she was tired enough to sleep for at least part of the night, but waking in the early hours of the morning there was nothing else to do but go over and over her problems.

The greatest of these, she quickly discovered, was how she was going to live without seeing the doctor each day. She supposed that she hadn't thought much about it before; he was always there, each day, and she had accepted that, not looking ahead. Even when she had supposed her heart to be broken by Charles there had always been the thought that the doctor was there, quiet in the background of her muddled mind.

He had become part of her life without her realising it and now there was nothing to be done about it. Falling in love, she discovered, wasn't anything like the infatuation she had had for Charles. It was the slow awareness of knowing that you wanted to be with someone for the rest of your life…

The days passed too quickly. She packed her small possessions, scoured the flat once more, said goodbye to Todd, and left the waiting room in a state of perfection and the filing cabinet in perfect order.

At the doctor's quiet request she presented herself with her case and Sam in his basket sharp on Saturday morning at nine o'clock. Somehow the leaving was made easier by the fact that he had told her to leave anything she wouldn't need at her aunt's, in the attic next to the flat. It seemed to her a kind of crack in the door, as it were.

With Sam grumbling in his basket on the back

seat and Bob beside him, they set off. The doctor had bidden her a cheerful good morning, observing that it should be a pleasant trip.

'I have always liked the late autumn,' he told
her, 'even though the days are short. You've
brought warm clothing with you? Miss West has
a charming house, and the village is just as
charming, but it is rather remote—though I believe there's a bus service to Ashburton once a
week.' He glanced sideways at her small profile
and added cheerfully, 'Probably you won't be
there long enough to try it out.'

'You haven't heard of anything that I could
do?' she asked, then added quickly, 'I'm sorry.
There was no need for me to say that. How can
you have had the time? I thought that if there is
nothing after a week or ten days I could go into
Exeter and look around for a job there.'

'A good idea,' said the doctor, not meaning
a word of it. He knew exactly what he was
going to do.

They stopped for coffee at a small wayside café on the A303, and Bob, his legs out of plaster now, went for a careful walk. Sam in his basket, somnolent after a big breakfast, hardly stirred.

It was impossible to feel unhappy; the man she had discovered that she loved was here beside her. Perhaps after today she might not see him again, but just for the moment she was happy. They didn't talk much, but when they did it was to discover that they liked the same things—the country, books, animals, winter evenings by the fire, walking in the moonlight. Oh, I do hope Mrs Seward likes the same things, thought Loveday. I want him to be happy.

They stopped for lunch at a hotel a few miles short of Exeter and then went on their way again—on the Plymouth road now, until they reached Ashburton and turned away from the main road and presently reached the village.

Miss West had the door open before the doctor

had stopped the car in front of it. He got out, opened Loveday's door and tucked her hand in his. 'Your niece Loveday, Miss West,' he said.

CHAPTER FIVE

LOVEDAY had grown more and more silent the nearer they had got to Buckland-in-the Moor. It had been a grey overcast day, and once they had left Ashburton behind the moor had stretched before them, magnificent and remote. She had had the nasty feeling that she shouldn't have come; her aunt might not like her, the doctor might not be able to find her another job and, worst of all, she might never see him again.

The lane they'd been driving along had taken a sharp bend and there before them had been the village, tucked beside the river Dart, and as though there had been a prearranged signal a beam of watery sunshine had escaped from the cloud.

'It's beautiful,' Loveday had said, and had suddenly felt much better. She'd turned to look at the doctor.

'I knew you would like it, Loveday,' he had said quietly, but he hadn't looked as he'd driven into the cluster of cottages, past the church, and stopped at Miss West's house.

She'd said in sudden panic, 'You won't go...?'

'No, I shall spend the night at the pub and drive back tomorrow.'

She had let out a small sigh of relief and got out when he'd opened her door, then stood for a moment looking at her aunt's home. There was no front garden, only a grass verge, and at this time of year the grey stone walls looked bleak and unwelcoming, but she had forgotten that when the door had opened and her aunt had stood there with a welcome warm enough to cheer the faintest heart.

Now in the narrow hall, she stopped to study Loveday. 'Your mother had green eyes,' she observed. 'I'm glad that we shall have the chance to get to know each other. You may call me Aunt Leticia.'

She turned to the doctor. 'You had a good journey?' She looked past him. 'The cat and your dog? They are in the car?'

'A very pleasant drive. Bob and Sam are in the car.'

'Good. There is a conservatory leading from the kitchen; Sam may go there for the moment. There is food—everything that he may need. Bob may come into the sitting room.'

She was urging Loveday before her and said over her shoulder, 'Her cases can wait; we will have tea. Take your coats off.'

Loveday did as she was told, and the doctor, amused, did the same, with a nostalgic memory of a fierce, much loved nanny speaking to him in just such a voice.

They had tea, a proper tea, sitting at a round table under the windows while the dogs and cats lay in a companionable heap before the fire. Presently a cautious Sam crept in and joined them, and since none of the animals did more than open an eye he settled down with all the appearance of someone who had come home…

The doctor fetched the cases presently and took his leave, but not before Aunt Leticia had bidden him to Sunday lunch.

'I attend Matins on Sunday mornings,' she told him, 'but I'm sure that you and Loveday will wish to discuss her future. A good walk in the fresh air will do you both good. Fetch her at ten o'clock. You can walk across to Holne and have coffee there. Lunch will be at one o'clock and then she and I will go to Evensong.'

The doctor, recognising an ally, agreed meekly, thanked the old lady for his tea, said a cheerful goodnight to Loveday and took himself and Bob off to the pub, where he was welcomed like an old friend. And later, after a good supper and a quick walk with Bob, he went to bed and slept the sleep of a man untroubled by his future.

* * *

Loveday, having repressed a strong desire to run out of the house after him, followed her aunt upstairs to a little room overlooking the back garden and the moor beyond. It was austerely furnished, and had the look of not having had an occupant for a long time, but there were books on the bedside table and a vase of chrysanthemums on the old-fashioned dressing table, and when she was left to unpack her things and opened the wardrobe and stiff drawers there was the delightful scent of lavender.

She went downstairs presently and helped to feed the cats and Tim, surprised to find that Sam seemed quite at home.

'I have always found animals better friends than people,' said Aunt Leticia, 'and they know that. When you go into the garden take care; there is a family of hedgehogs in the compost heap and rabbits in the hedge.'

They spent a pleasant evening together, looking at old photos of family Loveday scarcely remembered, and then, over their supper, Miss West began asking careful questions.

Loveday, enjoying the luxury of having someone to talk to, told her about Miss Cattell and then the doctor. Talking about him made him seem nearer, and her aunt, looking at her niece's ordinary face, saw how it lighted up when she talked of him.

Well, reflected Miss West, Loveday was an ice child. No looks worth mentioning, but with eyes like that looks didn't matter. The doctor was a good deal older, of course, but she didn't think that would matter in the least. He was clearly in love and suspected that Loveday was too, but for some reason she was denying it, even to herself. Ah, well, thought Miss West wisely, all that's needed is a little patience—and absence makes the heart grow fonder…

Loveday, with Sam for company, slept dreamlessly. Her last thoughts had been of the doctor and were the first on waking too. He would go away today, but there was the morning first...

She got up, dressed and went downstairs. She helped get the breakfast and saw to the animals and her aunt, who had liked her on sight, found the liking turning to affection. Loveday was a sensible girl who made no fuss and helped around the house without making a song and dance about it. She'll make Dr Fforde a good wife, reflected Aunt Leticia.

The doctor knocked on the door at ten o'clock, and after a few minutes chatting with Miss West he marched Loveday off at a brisk pace. Bob had come with him but he had already had a walk and now he was sitting contentedly in the sitting room with Tim. As the doctor explained, a long walk would be too tiring for his weak legs.

'Holne is about a mile away,' he told Loveday as they took the narrow road past the church. 'I'm told that we can get coffee there at the pub.

Then we can follow the river towards Wide-combe. There's a path.'

He began to talk about everything and nothing, with not a word about the future, and because she was so happy with him she forgot for the moment that she had no future and chatted away about the dogs and cats and the hedgehogs in the garden.

'I do like my aunt,' she told him. 'It must be difficult for her to have me living with her, even for a few days; she's lived alone for a long time and she told me that she was happy to be on her own. I expect she knows everyone in the vil-lage—she doesn't seem lonely.'

'I'm sure she will enjoy your company. Here's Holne and the pub—shall we stop for coffee?'

The coffee was excellent and there was a great log fire in the bar, but they didn't stay too long. They took the path close to the river and now it was the doctor's turn to tell her about his own life. Oh, yes, he told her when she asked, he had a mother, living in Lincolnshire where his father had had a practice before he died. 'And sisters,' he went on. 'You have met Margaret at the consulting room.'

Loveday came to a halt. 'I thought that she—that you—well, I thought you were going to marry her.'

She went red, although she looked him in the face.

He didn't allow himself to smile. So that was why she had pokered up... Another obstacle out of the way, he reflected. First Charles and now this. The temptation to take her in his arms there and then was great, but there was one more obstacle—the difference in their ages. He must give her time to think about that...

He said lightly, 'I've always been too busy to get married.' They were walking on now. 'And you, Loveday, have you no wish to marry?'

'Yes, but only to the right man.' She didn't want to talk about that. 'Do you suppose we should be turning back?'

He accepted her change in the conversation without comment.

They walked back the way they had come and the chilly bright morning began to cloud over. When they were within sight of the cottage, Loveday said, 'You will let me know…? I'm sorry to keep reminding you, but I'd like to be certain.'

'I promise you that I will let you know, and now that we are no longer working together could you not call me Andrew?'

She smiled suddenly. 'I've always called you Andrew inside my head,' she told him.

Lunch was a cheerful meal. Aunt Leticia might live alone, but she was aware of all that went on in the world so far removed from her home. There was plenty to talk about—until she said reluctantly, 'You will want to be on your way, and I mustn't keep you. Loveday, get your coat and walk up to the pub and see Dr Fforde safely away.'

The walk was short—far too short. Only a matter of a couple of minutes. Loveday stood by the car while the doctor invited Bob onto the back seat, closed the car door and turned to her.

He took her hands in his and stood looking down at her. The scarf she had tied over her mousy locks had done nothing to enhance her appearance. She looked about sixteen years old, and the last obstacle, the difference in their ages, was suddenly very real. He would marry her, but not until she had had the chance to lead her own life to meet people—young men—who would make her laugh as Charles had done.

All the things he wanted to say were unsaid. He wished her goodbye and got into the car and drove away.

She watched it through tear-filled eyes until it disappeared round the curve in the lane. Just for a moment she had thought that he was going to say something—that he would see her again, that they would keep in touch, remain friends...

She wiped her eyes and went back to Aunt Leticia. She helped with the washing up and then took the elderly Tim for his ambling walk, and later went to Evensong with her aunt. No one, looking at her quiet face, would have guessed how unhappy she was.

The days which followed were quiet, centred round the simple life Aunt Leticia lived, but there was always something to do. She often walked to Holne, a mile away, where there was a Post Office, and to the nearby farm for eggs, and halfway through each week she was sent to Ashburton on the weekly bus, armed with a shopping list—groceries and meat, wool for her aunt's knitting, and food for the cats and Tim. There was the weekly excitement of the travelling library, and the daily collecting of the newspapers from the pub.

The landlord liked a good gossip in his slow friendly voice; he was too kind a man to ask questions, but life in the village was quiet and her arrival had made a nice little break now that there were no visitors passing through. He had taken to the doctor, too, and had several times confided in his wife that there was more to his visits than met the eye…

It was late on a Saturday evening by the time the doctor arrived at the pub. It was too late to call on Miss West, so it was early on Sunday morning when Loveday got up to let Tim and the cats out and saw him coming down the lane.

She ran to the door and flung it wide as he reached it, and went into his arms with the unselfconsciousness of a child.

He closed the door gently behind them and then wrapped his arms around her again.

'I had to come. I had to know. You see, my darling Loveday, I'm in love with you…'

'Then why didn't you say so?' she asked fiercely.

'I'm so much older than you, and you have never had the chance to meet men of your own age. Only Charles.'

She dismissed Charles with a sniff. 'Is that your only reason?' She hesitated. 'I'm dull and plain and not at all clever. I'd be a very unexciting wife for someone like you.'

'I find you very exciting,' he told her, and kissed her, and presently said, 'You shall have all the time in the world to decide if you will marry me. I'll go back to London this evening and not come again until you can give me an answer.'

She looked at him then, and said in a shaky little voice, 'I'll stay here as long as you want me to, but I'll give you my answer now. I love you too, and I'll marry you—today if we could.'

He looked down at her earnest, loving face and smiled. Fourteen years were nothing; they simply didn't matter. He kissed her again, very thoroughly—a delightful experience which, naturally enough, was repeated.

Aunt Leticia, coming downstairs to put the kettle on made no effort to disturb them. Putting tea leaves into the teapot, she reflected that she would give them the silver pot which had belonged to her great-great-grandmother for a wedding present. She took her tea and sat by the Aga, waiting patiently. Let them have their lovely moment.